Braving Mussoorie's Madding Crowd

Ruskin Bond is known for his signature simplistic and witty writing style. He is the author of several bestselling short stories, novellas, collections, essays and children's books; and has contributed a number of poems and articles to various magazines and anthologies. At the age of twenty-three, he won the prestigious John Llewellyn Rhys Prize for his first novel, *The Room on the Roof*. He was also the recipient of the Padma Shri in 1999, Lifetime Achievement Award by the Delhi Government in 2012, and the Padma Bhushan in 2014.

Born in 1934, Ruskin Bond grew up in Jamnagar, Shimla, New Delhi and Dehradun. Apart from three years in the UK, he has spent all his life in India, and now lives in Landour, Mussoorie, with his adopted family.

By the same author:

Angry River
A Little Night Music
A Long Walk for Bina
Hanuman to the Rescue
Ghost Stories from the Raj
Strange Men, Strange Places
The India I Love
Tales and Legends from India
The Blue Umbrella
Ruskin Bond's Children's Omnibus
The Ruskin Bond Omnibus-I
The Ruskin Bond Omnibus-II
The Ruskin Bond Omnibus-III
The Rupa Book of Great Animal Stories
The Rupa Book of True Tales of Mystery and Adventure
The Rupa Book of Ruskin Bond's Himalayan Tales
The Rupa Book of Great Suspense Stories
The Rupa Laughter Omnibus
The Rupa Book of Scary Stories
The Rupa Book of Haunted Houses
The Rupa Book of Travellers' Tales
The Rupa Book of Great Crime Stories
The Rupa Book of Nightmare Tales
The Rupa Book of Shikar Stories
The Rupa Book of Love Stories
The Rupa Book of Wicked Stories
The Rupa Book of Heartwarming Stories
The Rupa Book of Thrills and Spills

Braving Mussoorie's Madding Crowd

Selected and Compiled by
RUSKIN BOND

Published by
Rupa Publications India Pvt. Ltd 2020
7/16, Ansari Road, Daryaganj
New Delhi 110002

Sales centres:
Bengaluru Chennai
Hyderabad Jaipur Kathmandu
Kolkata Mumbai Prayagraj

Copyright © Ruskin Bond 2020

This is a work of fiction. Names, characters, places and incidents are either the product of the author's imagination or are used fictitiously and any resemblance to any actual person, living or dead, events or locales is entirely coincidental.

All rights reserved.
No part of this publication may be reproduced, transmitted, or stored in a retrieval system, in any form or by any means, electronic, mechanical, photocopying, recording or otherwise, without the prior permission of the publisher.

P-ISBN: 978-93-5333-805-3
E-ISBN: 978-93-5333-806-0

Fourth impression 2025

10 9 8 7 6 5 4

Printed in India

This book is sold subject to the condition that it shall not, by way of trade or otherwise, be lent, resold, hired out, or otherwise circulated, without the publisher's prior consent, in any form of binding or cover other than that in which it is published.

Contents

Introduction	ix
Cheese	1
By Jerome K. Jerome	
Ong to Londing	6
A Question	7
The Conjurer's Revenge	8
By Stephen Leacock	
Llanfairpwllgwyngillgogerchwyrn drobwllllandysiliogogogoch	11
By Robert Lynd	
The Kidnapping of Major Mulvaney	16
By C.A. Kincaid	
Money	35
By Richard Armour	
Cricket at Dingley Dell	36
By Charles Dickens	
Cricket—Field Placings	43
The Cricket Match	44
By A.G. Macdonnel	

Major Canamus	54
By A.G. Shirreff	
George and Ranji	63
The Zigzag Walk	66
The Decline of the Drama	69
By Stephen Leacock	
Pause	75
By Pierre Marivaux	
Sigh No More, Ladies	76
By Thomas Percy	
Drunkards of Distinction	77
Company	83
By Aimor A. Dickson	
Wimpole's Woe	84
By Louis Golding	
My Failed Omelettes—and Other Disasters	91
Song for a Beetle in a Goldfish Bowl	94
The Inn and the Dog	96
By Jerome K. Jerome	
The Ghost Ship	105
By Richard Middleton	
About John Who Lost a Fortune by Throwing Stones	118
By Hilaire Belloc	
Henry King	122
By Hilaire Belloc	
Matilda	123
By Hilaire Belloc	

The Dinner-Party	125
By E.V. Lucas	
The Faith Cure	132
By A.G. Shirreff	
A Comedy in Capricorn	136
By Morley Roberts	
Ping Pong & Ruskin Bond	161
By Victor Banerjee	
The Music Man	167
By Vijay N. Shankar	
In Praise of the Sausage	172
Last Tango in the Far Pavilions	174
By Bill Aitken	
Literacy Lapses	178
Verses: From the Sanskrit	179
By A.G. Shirreff	
When I Smelt a Rat, and Gave Up Chocolate	181
Braving Mussoorie's Madding Crowd	184
Why I Miss the Good Old GP Who Kept it Simple	187
Why I Miss My Less-Cash Days	190
On Losing Solitude, and Discovering the Joy of Selfies	193
Belting around Mumbai	196
Monkey on the Roof	199
And in the Loo	205
And at the Bank	212
Granny's Tree-Climbing	219

Introduction

Dear Reader,

The pen (we are told) is mightier than the sword; I'm not sure about that, but it's certainly easier to write with....

Frankly, given a choice of writing weapons, I would always choose the pen in preference to the typewriter, the word-processor, the tape-recorder, or the secretary. On one occasion I spent over an hour dictating to a tape-recorder only to discover later that I had forgotten to switch it on. A word-processor took one of my stories and vanished with it forever. A secretary took one of my best friends and vanished with him forever.

An expensive pen may occasionally vanish, depending on the company you keep, but an inexpensive ball-point seldom lets me down. I keep a bunch of these handy: some on my desk, two or three in my coat pockets, one under my pillow, one near the telephone, a couple in convenient flower-pots (I get the occasional bright idea while gardening), and one in the kitchen just in case I decide to write that cookery book which is going to make my fortune. Pens accompany me on long walks. Computers don't, and secretaries won't.

In compiling this collection of humorous stories, sketches, and verse, I have enjoyed myself immensely. I have been able to revive a few old favourites, discover or re-discover others, and give you, my dear reader, something to smile or laugh at on a gloomy or rainy day.

There are basically three kinds of humour: wit, satire, comedy. The wit (in the manner of Wilde, Shaw, etc.) is funny at the expense of other people; the satirist is funny at the expense of the world; the comedian is funny at his own expense, or he sees the funny side of human existence.

Wit and satire are inclined to fade, just as the subjects of their barbs fade away, lose their immediacy and relevance. Great comedy is immortal. Shakespeare's Falstaff and Dickens's Mr Micawber never cease to enchant. These and others like them are larger than life, just as Chaplin's tramp is their visual equivalent: converting human frailty into something laughable, loveable. The perfect example of a writer able to laugh at his own foibles and follies is Jerome K. Jerome, in his classic, *Three Men in a Boat,* and its sequel, *Three Men on the Bummel.* Gifted humourists in their different ways were Stephen Leacock, Morley Roberts, Hilaire Belloc, P.G. Wodehouse. They have made the world a better place, simply by making us laugh at them, with them, and at ourselves.

I am grateful to a few friends for contributing to this anthology: Vijay N. Shankar, a newspaper editor who also writes fiction; the actor Victor Banerjee, who takes a mischievous look at some of your editor's hidden talents; and Bill Aitken, the well-known travel writer.

The poems by A.G. Shirreff appear here for the first time since their original, unheralded publication in 1918. It always gives me pleasure to re-discover a forgotten or neglected writer whose work deserves to be read again.

Kipling was only occasionally humorous, but in one of his

stories he said that in order to survive in India you needed a strong sense of humour. I would go further and say that in order to survive anywhere in today's world, you need to have a pretty good sense of humour.

May this book help you to look at the funny side of life. And as Dr Johnson said, "Laugh and be well!"

Ruskin Bond

Cheese

By *Jerome K. Jerome*

There is too much odour about cheese. I remember a friend of mine buying a couple of cheeses at Liverpool.

Splendid cheeses they were, ripe and mellow, and with a two hundred horsepower scent about them that might have been warranted to carry three miles, and knock a man over at two hundred yards. I was in Liverpool at the time, and my friend said that if I didn't mind he would get me to take them back with me to London, as he should not be coming up for a day or two himself, and he did not think the cheeses ought to be kept much longer.

'Oh, with pleasure, dear boy' I replied, 'with pleasure.'

I called for the cheeses, and took them away in a cab. It was a ramshackle affair, dragged along by a knock-kneed, broken-winded somnambulist, which his owner, in a moment of enthusiasm during conversation, referred to as a horse. I put the cheeses on the top, and we started off at a shamble that would have done credit to the swiftest steam-roller ever built, and all went merry as a funeral bell, until we turned the corner. There, the wind carried a whiff from the cheeses full on to our steed. It woke him up, and, with a snort of terror, he dashed off at three miles an hour. The wind still blew in his direction, and before we reached the end of the street he was laying himself out at the rate of nearly four miles an hour, leaving the cripples and stout old ladies nowhere.

It took two porters as well as the driver to hold him at the station; and I do not think they would have done it, even then, had not one of the men had the presence of mind to put a handkerchief over his nose, and to light a bit of brown paper.

I took my ticket, and marched proudly up the platform, with my cheeses, the people falling back respectfully on either side. The train was crowded, and I had to get into a carriage where there were already seven other people. One crusty old gentleman objected, but I got in, notwithstanding; and, putting my cheeses upon the rack, squeezed down with a pleasant smile, and said it was a warm day. A few moments passed, and then the old gentleman began to fidget.

Very close in here,' he said. 'Quite oppressive,' said the man next him.

And then they both began sniffing, and, at the third sniff they caught it right on the chest, and rose up without another word and went out. And then a stout lady got up, and said it was disgraceful that a respectable married woman should be harried about in this way, and gathered up a bag and eight parcels and went. The remaining four passengers sat on for a while, until a solemn looking man in the corner who, from his dress and general appearance, seemed to belong to the undertaker class, said it put him in mind of a dead baby; and the other three passengers tried to get out of the door at the same time, and hurt themselves.

I smiled at the gentleman in black, and said I thought we were going to have the carriage to ourselves, and he laughed pleasantly, and said that some people made such a fuss over a little thing. But even he grew strangely depressed after we had started, and so, when we reached Crewe, I asked him to come and have a drink. He accepted, and we forced our way into the buffet, where we yelled, and stamped, and waved our umbrellas for a quarter of an hour; and then a young lady came and asked us if we wanted anything.

'What's yours?' I said, turning to my friend.

'I'll have half-a-crown's worth of brandy, neat, if you please, miss,' he responded.

And he went off quietly after he had drunk it and got into another carriage, which I thought mean.

From Crewe I had the compartment to myself, though the train was crowded. As we drew up at the different stations, the people, seeing my empty carriage, would rush for it. 'Here y'are, Maria; come along, plenty of room.' 'All right, Tom; we'll get in here,' they would shout. And they would run along, carrying heavy bags, and fight round the door to get in first. And one would open the door and mount the steps, and stagger back into the arms of the man behind him; and they would all come and have a sniff, and then drop off and squeeze into other carriages, or pay the difference and go first.

From Euston, I took the cheeses down to my friend's house. When his wife came into the room she smelt round for an instant. Then she said:

'What is it? Tell me the worst.' I said:

'It's cheeses. Tom bought them in Liverpool, and asked me to bring them up with me.'

And I added that I hoped she understood that it had nothing to do with me; and she said that she was sure of that, but that she would speak to Tom about it when he came back.

My friend was detained in Liverpool longer than he expected

and, three days later, as he hadn't returned home, his wife called on me. She said:

'What did Tom say about those cheeses?'

I replied that he had directed they were to be kept in a moist place, and that nobody was to touch them.

She said:

'Nobody's likely to touch them. Had he smelt them?'

I thought he had, and added that he seemed greatly attached to them.

You think he would be upset, she queried, 'if I gave a man a sovereign to take them away and bury them?'

I answered that I thought that he would never smile again. An idea struck her. She said:

'Do you mind keeping them for him? Let me send them round to you.

'Madam,' I replied, 'for myself I like the smell of cheese, and the journey the other day with them from Liverpool I shall ever look back upon as a happy ending to a pleasant holiday. But, in this world, we must consider others. The lady under whose roof I have the honour of residing is a widow, and, for all I know, possibly an orphan too. She has a strong, I may say, an eloquent, objection to being what she terms "put upon". The presence of your husband's cheeses in her house she would, I instinctively feel, regard as a "put upon"; and it shall never be said that I put upon the widow and the orphan.'

'Very well, then,' said my friend's wife, rising, 'all I have to say is, that I shall take the children and go to a hotel until those cheeses are eaten. I decline to live any longer in the same house with them.'

She kept her word, leaving the place in charge of the charwoman, who, when asked if she could stand the smell, replied, 'What smell?' and who, when taken close to the cheeses and told to sniff hard, said she could detect a faint odour of melons. It was argued from this that little injury could result to the woman from the atmosphere, and she was left.

The hotel bill came to fifteen guineas; and my friend, after reckoning everything up, found that the cheeses had cost him eight-and-sixpence a pound. He said he dearly loved a bit of cheese, but it was beyond his means; so he determined to get rid of them. He threw them into the canal; but had to fish them out again, as the bargemen complained. They said it made them feel quite faint. And, after that, he took them one dark night and left them in the parish mortuary. But the coroner discovered them, and made a fearful fuss.

He said it was a plot to deprive him of his living by waking up the corpses.

My friend got rid of them, at last, by taking them down to a seaside town, and burying them on the beach. It gained the place quite a reputation. Visitors said they had never noticed before how strong the air was, and weak-chested and consumptive people used to throng there for years afterwards.

From *Three Men In A Boat*

Ong to Londing

'Parding Mrs Harding,
Is my kitting in your garding,
Gnawing of a mutting-bone?'
'No, he's gone to Londing.'
'How many miles to Londing?
Eleving? I thought it was only seving.
Heavings! What a long way from home!'

                      Recalled from an old music-hall song

A Question

One day Soshi was walking on the bank of a river with a friend. 'How delightfully the fishes are enjoying themselves in the water!' exclaimed Soshi. His friend said: 'You are not a fish; how do you know that the fishes are enjoying themselves?' 'You are not myself,' returned Soshi; 'how do you know that I do not know that the fishes are enjoying themselves?'

From *The Book of Tea* by Kakuzo Okakura

The Conjurer's Revenge

By Stephen Leacock

'Now, ladies and gentlemen,' said the conjurer, 'having shown you that the cloth is absolutely empty, I will proceed to take from it a bowl of goldfish. Presto!' All round the hall people were saying, 'Oh, how wonderful! How does he do it?'

But the Quick Man on the front seat said in a big whisper to the people near him, 'He—had—it—up—his—sleeve.'

Then the people nodded brightly at the Quick Man and said, 'Oh, of course'; and everybody whispered round the hall, 'He had—it—up—his—sleeve.'

'My next trick,' said the conjurer, 'is the famous Hindustani rings. You will notice that the rings are apparently separate; at a blow they all join (clang, clang, clang)—Presto!'

There was a general buzz of stupefaction till the Quick Man was heard to whisper, 'He—must—have—had—another—lot up—his—sleeve.'

Again everybody nodded and whispered, 'The-rings were—up—his—sleeve.'

The brow of the conjurer was clouded with a gathering frown. 'I will now,' he continued, 'show you a most amusing trick by which I am enabled to take any number of eggs from a hat. Will some gentleman kindly lend me his hat? Ah, thank you—Presto!'

He extracted seventeen eggs, and for thirty-five seconds the audience began to think that he was wonderful. Then the Quick Man whispered along the front bench, 'He—has—a—hen—up—his—sleeve,' and all the people whispered it on. 'He—has—lot—of—hens—up—his—sleeve.'

The egg trick was ruined.

It went on like that all through. It transpired from the whispers of the Quick Man that the conjurer must have concealed up his sleeve, in addition to the rings, hens, and fish, several packs of cards, a loaf of bread, a doll's cradle, a live guinea-pig, a fifty cent piece, and a rocking-chair.

The reputation of the conjurer was rapidly sinking below zero. At the close of the evening he rallied for a final effort.

'Ladies and gentlemen,' he said, 'I will present to you in conclusion, the famous Japanese trick recently invented by the natives of Tipperary. Will you, sir,' he continued, turning towards the Quick Man, 'will you kindly hand me your gold watch?'

It was passed to him.

'Have I your permission to put it into this mortar and pound it to pieces?' he asked savagely.

The Quick Man nodded and smiled.

The conjurer threw the watch into the mortar and grasped a sledge-hammer from the table. There was a sound of violent smashing, 'He's—slipped—it—up—his—sleeve,' whispered the Quick Man.

'Now, sir,' continued the conjurer, 'will you allow me to take your handkerchief and punch holes in it? Thank you. You see, ladies and gentlemen, there is no deception; the holes are visible to the eye.'

The face of the Quick Man beamed. This time the real mystery of the thing fascinated him.

'And now, sir, will you kindly pass me your silk hat and allow me to dance on it? Thank you.'

The conjurer made a few rapid passes with his feet and exhibited the hat, crushed beyond recognition.

'And will you now, sir, take off your celluloid collar and permit me to burn it in the candle? Thank you, sir. And will you allow me to smash your spectacles for you with my hammer? Thank you.'

By this time the features of the Quick Man were assuming a puzzled expression. 'This thing beats me,' he whispered, I don't see through it a bit.'

There was a great hush upon the audience. Then the conjurer drew himself up to his full height and, with a withering look at the Quick Man, he concluded:

'Ladies and gentlemen, you will observe that I have, with this gentleman's permission, broken his watch, burnt his collar, smashed his spectacles, and danced on his hat. If he will give me the further permission to paint green stripes on his overcoat, or to tie his suspenders in a knot, I shall be delighted to entertain you. If not, the performance is at an end.'

Amid a glorious burst of music from the orchestra the curtain fell, and the audience dispersed, convinced that there are some tricks, at any rate, that are not done up the conjurer's sleeve.

Llanfairpwllgwyngillgogerchwyrndrob-wllllandysiliogogogoch

By Robert Lynd

That, according to a Welsh Member of Parliament, is not the right way to spell it. Two syllables of the name, he told the House of Commons, are here placed in the wrong order. Perhaps it was the misspelling that made the House so hilarious, when the name of the village was mentioned in a question addressed to the Postmaster-General. Every reader of *Punch* knows how funny even the most trifling mistake in spelling can be. At the same time, I suspect that in its correct spelling the name of Llanfairpwllgwyn, etc., would have seemed equally comic to Englishmen, and possibly to Welshmen. It is a dachshund of a word elongated almost to infinity, and even an ordinary dachshund is funny.

It is difficult to say at what point a word begins to grow funny because of its length. Remove one letter after another from the end of this Welsh word, and at what point will it cease to be funny! Take away the entire second half of the word, and it will still be ridiculous.

The Welsh are a race of bards, but I doubt if they have ever invented a metre which could contain the name of this village, the postmaster of which has given notice of his resignation. Even in free verse the word would look a little absurd. It scarcely looks right in a page of common prose.

The Welsh, I fancy, have preserved it mainly as an attraction for tourists. I am sure that no Welshman talking to another Welshman ever rolls out that horrid and disordered alphabet. No nation could survive which in its ordinary speech gave places names like that. In these days of keen competition, it is the race with the short words that wins. Names of undue length are an obstruction to business whether on the railways, in the post office, or in the houses of commerce. If you were ordering bulbs, and you were hesitating whether to order them from Tring or Llanfair, etc., etc., you would end by ordering them from Tring merely in order to save trouble.

Presumably, then, it was a Welsh humorist who invented the name in order to give visitors something to wonder at. If I remember right, when I was in Wales many years ago, you could buy the name on a sheet of paper for a penny, and, if you were a stranger, you did. It was a curiosity, worthy of being added to the seven wonders of the world. It was more astonishing than Snowdon and more difficult to master.

It was Wales, too, in an ingratiatingly comic mood—Wales all but Rabelaisian. Presumably, it is the longest word in the world, and the longest word in the world is in its own way as interesting as the longest river in the world or the highest mountain or the largest lake. If you were told that the tallest tree in the world was in a Surrey wood, you would drive out to see it with the liveliest curiosity. You and thousands of others would stand gazing at it simply through a passion for the superlative. The superlatively big and the superlatively little—each of them stirs us into wonder. We should admire equally a Bible so huge that one had to climb a ladder to reach the top of the page, and a Bible so tiny that it could be fitted into a thimble. We are all victims of the love of the odd, and many people would go farther to see a man ten feet high or with three eyes than to talk with Socrates.

Yet always in the end we return for repose to the normal. An excess of excess wearies us. If all places had names like that of the unpronounceable Welsh village, we should be bored and not interested. The truth is, the name has no virtue but uniqueness, It is, as Johnson said of Gray, merely dull in a new way. It is as though a painter exhibited a picture which had no claim on our interest except that it was the largest picture, or the smallest picture, in the world. We might go to see it once, but not twice. We cannot say exactly what is the right size for a picture, but we know that there are limits of size in both directions beyond which a painter cannot go without peril of freakishness. It is the same with books. Some years ago writers discussed the question, 'What is the right length for a novel?' and many people though the question ridiculous. But it would have been ridiculous only if it had implied that an exact length could be discovered to which all novels should be expected to conform. In point of fact, it is clear that, in regard to the length of his novels, the novelist is bound by rules, however impossible these rules may be to formulate. It is safe to lay it down as a principle that no novel may be as long as the *Encyclopaedia Britannica* or as short as an ordinary postcard. At what point excessive length or excessive brevity begins, however, it is impossible to determine. Many people thought, probably rightly, that the novel in the nineties was becoming too short. Many people think, probably rightly, that the novel today is becoming too long again.

Even in our sentences we are bound by rules that forbid

alike excessive length and excessive brevity. If a newspaper were written in sentences each of which ran to a column, I doubt if it would have a single subscriber after the first number. If it were written in sentences none of which was more than three words long, it would be scarcely less tedious. The eye is comfortable only in travelling over normal stretches of words. It is as easily bewildered and confused by too many full-stops as by too few. Somewhere, but indefinable, are the limits of the normal, and between these exists all excellent writing.

And, as with sentences, so with words. At least, it is obvious that words cannot be too long without exciting the ridicule of ordinary human beings. I have heard it said that the longest word in the English language is 'disestablishmentarianism', but I doubt if this is true. I am sure the vocabulary of science contains worse examples of multiliteralism. If the jargon of science has often been ridiculed by comic writers, it is because men of science have been given to the use of words so long as to be meaningless to the ordinary eye. What can an ordinary man make of such a sentence (written by a botanist) as: 'The hydroid of a Pteridophyte or of a Phanerogram is characteristically a dead, usually elongated cell containing air and water, and either thin-walled with lignified (woody) spiral, or annular, thickenings, or with thick lignified walls, incompletely perforated by pits (usually bordered pits) of various shapes, e.g. the pits may be separated by a network of thickenings when the tracheid is *reticulate* or they may be transversely elongated and separated by bars of thickening like the rungs of a ladder (sculariform thickenings)?' What is to be made of 'microsporophylls' and 'macrosporopylls'. of "parenchymatous cortex' or a 'hydrom-stereom strand somewhat like that of the rhizome in other Polytrichaceae? Such a battery of long words stuns all but the determined student, and terrifies common men from approaching the domain of science. It is possible that a private jargon is necessary for every science, and that this is no more essentially ridiculous than foreign words, which frequently seem absurd to those who do not understand them. At the same time, I am sure the philosophers and men of science have used them oftener, than was necessary. They are like men taking pride in a national language. There is a vanity of language that expresses itself in polysyllables. Every science has its Llanfairpwllgwyngillgogerchwyrndrobwllllandysiliogogogochs and is proud of them.

And the curious thing is that these long words seldom mean anything half so important as ordinary people express in words of four or five letters. You can spell 'man' in three letters, but, if you want to name some invisible microbe lurking under his finger-nail, you will probably need a word containing twenty. Llanfairpwllgwyngillgogerchwyrndrobwllllandysiliogogogoch, which is an obscure village, has a name containing fifty-seven letters: Rome, a great and ancient city, is content with a name containing four. There is a moral in this. I wish I knew what it is.

The Kidnapping of Major Mulvaney

By C.A. Kincaid[1]

In his comfortable room on the first floor of the Bombay Secretariat offices, sat one January afternoon in the middle eighties the Honourable Mr George Massena Robinson, C.S.I., I.C.S., member of the Council of H. E. the Governor of Bombay. As he sat he swore horribly, and as he swore he read over and over again an official letter just received from the Political Agent of Kathiawar, a province divided up into a number of Indian States on the western seaboard of India. Then it was little known, but since it has become famous as the birthplace of the immortal 'Ranji'.

The letter ran as follows:

---

[1] Kincaid, a prolific writer, enjoyed a long career in the Indian Civil Service and was at one time Political Agent of Kathiawar.

26th January 1885

From Major Mulvaney,
Assistant Political Agent of Jetalsar.

To:
The Secretary to the Government of Bombay,
Political Department.

Sir,

In continuation of my letter of the 11th instant, I have the honour to inform you that since you sent no reply to it, the dacoit Naja Wala has cut off my right ear. I have the honour to send it, herewith enclosed. He further threatens to cut off my left ear if the rupees thirty thousand demanded are not paid within a fortnight. He will follow up this outrage by cutting my throat. In these circumstances I sincerely hope that His Excellency in Council will pay my ransom and rescue me from my present unenviable situation.

                    I have the honour to be,
                              Sir,
                    Your most obedient servant
                         Patrick Mulvaney,
                              (Major)

One enclosure—the right ear of Major Mulvaney, in sealed envelope.

Submitted through the Political Agent.

Forwarded with compliments. The Undersigned trusts that

Government will take the necessary steps to release this unfortunate officer.

John Haslop,
Political Agent.

Kathiawar, 27th January.

Mr Robinson looked back through the file and discovered the letter to which Major Mulvaney had referred. It had come when Mr Robinson had been on tour and had been kept several days to await his return and was marked "Immediate". The letter stated briefly that Major Mulvaney had been touring in the Jornagar State on inspection duty. As he was riding in that part of the great Kathiawar forest known as the Gir, that lay in Jornagar State, a certain Kathi outlaw called Naja Wala, accompanied by ten or twelve kinsmen, had surrounded and kidnapped him. Naja Wala was holding him to ransom for thirty thousand rupees. Failing the payment of the ransom, the outlaw threatened to cut off Major Mulvaney's right ear and send it to the Bombay Government to show that he meant business. Major Mulvaney trusted that the said Government would pay the money and secure his release, since he had been on duty when captured. On this letter the office had noted that they had consulted the Accountant General's office, but had learnt that no fund existed for the payment of ransom for British officers. No action, therefore, seemed called for. The Under Secretary agreed and added that Major Mulvaney might be informed that although the Government could take no action, His Excellency in Council would hear with pleasure that Major Mulvaney had been able to raise the ransom among his friends and brother officers. The Secretary would gladly have concurred but he had recently been warned that it was his duty to record his own opinion and not merely to initial his subordinates' remarks. He therefore struck out an independent line. He suggested that the thirty thousand rupees earmarked in the budget for four bridges and a resthouse in the Dharwar district should be reappropriated towards payment of Major Mulvaney's ransom.

The Honourable Mr Robinson minuted that nothing could be done for Major Mulvaney and that he should be so informed on the lines so well indicated by the Under Secretary. Having disposed of this "immediate" file the Honourable member took up his favourite newspaper, the *Bombay Gazette*. To his utter disgust he read in the first leading article an account of Major Mulvaney's misfortunes. At its close the editor asked rhetorically how long that gallant officer would have to await his liberation. He had lost one ear, the editor understood, was he to lose the other ear and his eyes and nose as well?

"The cowardly poltroon!" groaned Mr Robinson. "Not satisfied with getting himself kidnapped, he is now raising a press campaign against the Government!" Then he looked disgustedly at the ear which he had taken out of its envelope and muttered: "It's quite black: the fellow's nothing but a damned halfcaste!"

After this outburst the Honourable Mr Robinson re-opened the Major Mulvaney file, scored through his previous minute and wrote that he approved the admirable suggestion of the Secretary. The Dharwar district had waited so long for the bridges and the resthouse that it could well wait another year. A telegram should be sent to the Political Agent and he should be instructed to inform Naja Wala that the ransom would be paid at the earliest opportunity, provided that no further injury were done to Major Mulvaney. The Political Agent sent the contents of the telegram to the Jornagar State, who contrived to communicate them to Naja Wala.

At the close of the day's work the Honourable Mr Robinson wrote to the private secretary and asked him with His Excellency's permission to put a black mark against Major Mulvaney's name. He should be told that he could expect no further promotion in view of the expense to which he had put the Bombay Government through his carelessness and indifference to their interests. Having written this vicious little note, the Honourable Mr Robinson forgot his worries and went back happily to his house on the ridge of Malabar Hill.

Now let us leave the Honourable Mr George Robinson and introduce ourselves to Major Mulvaney, Assistant Political Agent of Jetalsar and the cause of so much annoyance to the Bombay Government. Originally a lieutenant in the 160th Marathas, he had grown tired—for he was extremely lazy—of the routine of an Indian regiment and had used such influence as he possessed to get himself posted to the Bombay political department. He had now been some twelve years a political officer and in his new career, as it must be admitted, he had succeeded quite well. He had not disposed of many cases, but that did not matter much; for no litigation in Kathiawar is ever finally decided. On the other hand he had an Irishman's pleasant manner and his uncanny knack of understanding the Indian, a gift usually denied to the Englishman. If the Political Agent found one of his chiefs difficult or obstinate, he had only to send Major Mulvaney to see him. That gallant officer would invariably worm out of the chief his real objections and meet them. The Political Agent had in fact a warm regard for Major Mulvaney and was shocked to think that his valuable subordinate was in the hands of a Kathi brigand and in mortal peril.

He need not, however, have felt as anxious as he did. Major Mulvaney was in no danger; for the facts that underlay his capture by the Kathi Naja Wala were as follows:

Like most Irishmen, Major Mulvaney was fond of horses and of horse races. Some two years before the date of his capture he had gone to Bombay to stay with his friend, the Editor of the *Bombay Gazette*, for ten days. He had attended the Bombay race meeting and had betted at first in moderation. He was an excellent judge of horseflesh and by sheer good judgment had spotted half a dozen winners in succession. So elated was the gallant Major that he backed his opinion recklessly. On one animal he staked no less than ten thousand rupees. To Mulvaney's experienced eyes it seemed the best horse in the paddock and indeed so it was. Unfortunately he reckoned without its owner. The latter had praised it to all his friends as a 'dead cert' and then had secretly laid against it for all he was worth. Under his instructions the jockey skilfully lost the race. Nowadays owner and jockey would have been warned off for pulling; but in the eighties the stewards were neither so strict nor so competent. The owner collected his ill-gotten gains and left Bombay hurriedly. The unfortunate Mulvaney found himself some nine thousand rupees down at the end of the meeting and his total assets did not exceed five hundred. There was nothing for him to do but to go to a firm of Marwadis, the moneylending caste of India, borrow the money and pay the bookies. Mulvaney was no fool and he borrowed the money with great reluctance, for he guessed that the door of the Marwadi's shop was the first step on the road to ruin. Still there was no other course open to him. He borrowed nine thousand rupees, signed a document for twelve thousand, a reference to two arbitrators and finally a decree embodying their decision. The meaning of these various papers was that if Major Mulvaney did not pay back twelve thousand rupees at the end of a year, the Marwadis would have ready to their hand a consent decree for that sum. They would not have to sue their debtor. They would merely have to execute a consent decree against him. Marwadis do not lend money as an ordinary business transaction, but to squeeze their debtors dry.

Major Mulvaney did his best to collect the twelve thousand rupees so as to repay the Marwadis at the end of the year; but it was hopeless. His total pay was eight hundred rupees a month and he would have had to save a thousand a month to do so. At the end of the year the Marwadi's agent appeared at Jetalsar and demanded the money under threat of immediate execution. Major Mulvaney had scraped together three thousand five hundred and offered that sum in part payment. He asked for time; but the agent refused point blank. At last he affected to be touched by Mulvaney's pleadings and consented to enter two thousand five hundred rupees on the decree. The other thousand were set aside to cover the agent's expenses. Major Mulvaney felt at first some slight relief; but it vanished when it was pointed out to him that, although the capital sum had been reduced, he had, under the terms of the bond, to go on paying on the entire twelve thousand interest at thirty per cent until the last rupee had been paid off. Now 30 per cent on twelve thousand is 3,600 rupees a year or three hundred rupees a month, so that it became really impossible for the debtor ever to pay off his debt. He was fairly caught in the Marwadis' net. After a year of hopeless indebtedness the Irishman's fertile brain began to look for some way out of the road to Hell down which he was steadily proceeding. He wrote home to his elder brother Mr Thaddeus Mulvaney of Mulvaney Castle for financial assistance. The latter had a large landed estate on the Sligo coast, with a nominal rentroll of £2,000 a year. But it was only nominal like most Irish rentrolls. The tenants rarely paid more than a quarter of their rents. On the other hand they poached the river and the grouse moors so that they could not be let. Indeed if Mr Thaddeus Mulvaney collected from his farmers five hundred pounds in twelve months, he thought that he had done rather well. When, therefore, he got a letter from his younger brother Patrick, asking him for a loan of nine hundred pounds so as to liquidate his debt for twelve thousand rupees, he whistled and then shrugged his shoulders. He doubted whether he could have raised nine hundred pence at a moment's notice. Still he was fond of his brother Patrick and he advised him to shake the dust of India from off his feet and return to dear old Ireland. Once there Thaddeus hoped that he could secure for him the post of a resident magistrate or some similar office. Anyway, Patrick could always live at Mulvaney Castle and work as Thaddeus' land agent. The latter was a bachelor and even lazier than his young brother. But Patrick must find his own way to Ireland, as there was no money to be had in the castle either from Thaddeus or anyone else.

When Major Mulvaney read his brother's reply, he felt no great disappointment. He had feared that Thaddeus would have no cash to send him; but when he thought of the indolent life in Ireland with the rich meadows at the castle door and the great Atlantic rollers breaking close by on the Sligo coast, he felt overcome with homesickness and he longed to be rid of India and the Marwadis' slave chain. What career had he in front of him? After paying them their pound of flesh every month he had only just enough left to keep himself alive. He could never put money by for a trip home or even to Bombay. Sooner or later the Government would hear he was in debt and would not promote him. For the rule was strict. Officers in high places must be free from debt and, therefore, not exposed to temptations. If only he could raise money for a ticket to England; but it was a hopeless proposition. So Major Mulvaney sat huddled up in an armchair in his verandah at Jetalsar, looking at the sun-baked landscape across which a fresh cold wind was blowing. Then suddenly he had a brainwave.

When he had last been on leave Major Mulvaney had landed at 'Gib and had gone to the regimental mess to meet one or two old friends and have a drink. There he had heard an amazing tale that had much interested him. It appeared that in Tangier there lived a Mr Henderson, the correspondent of the *Standard* newspaper, and a certain Scotch adventurer called Kaid Macintosh, the Commander-in-chief of the army of the Sultan of Morocco. Both were inveterate gamblers and very hard up; so to raise the wind they had induced a Berber brigand named Haji Isa Khan, whom they knew, to carry them off to the Atlas mountains and hold them to ransom. The Haji was willing to oblige two old friends and took them off one day from Mr Henderson's villa outside Tangier. Before he left Henderson sent off a telegram to the *Standard*, informing the editor of his own and his friend's fate. A press campaign for their release followed with the result that under pressure from the British Government the Sultan paid £30,000 for the release of the two captives. The honest brigand let them go, paying to each of them ten thousand pounds. The balance he kept himself.

This tale suddenly flashed across Major Mulvaney's brain and he asked himself why he should not do something of the same kind himself. Of course he would not ask for thirty thousand pounds. The Bombay Government would never pay such a sum; but he might be held to ransom for thirty thousand rupees. This amount the Government might pay and he and his captor might share the money. With the modest sum so realised he would be able to get home and have a few hundred pounds in hand until he got a job of some kind.

'Now who could I get to kidnap me?' muttered Mulvaney half aloud. 'Yes, by Jove, there is one likely fellow, Naja Wala of Sudodhra.' The man in question was a Kathi[2] landholder of the Jornagar State. Major Mulvaney had first met him some three years before, when he had gone into outlawry, because the Jornagar administration had imposed a new tax on his holding. The sum involved was only two rupees or three shillings a year; but such was the touchiness of the Kathi gentleman that, sooner than pay what he thought an unjust tax, he abandoned his house and lands and he and his kinsmen became brigands. Major Mulvaney understood, as an Irishman, the Kathi's injured pride and handled him in just the right way. He arranged that the chief of Jornagar should give up the tax and accept as a present the gift of a Kathi mare. The mare came of a famous stock and was worth at least a thousand rupees; but she was a voluntary offering that Naja Wala was proud to make. On the other hand he would have killed himself rather than pay an increased impost on his hereditary lands; for his family had held them long before Jornagar had become a ruling state.

Major Mulvancey sent a polite note to Naja Wala begging him to call on him at Jetalsar. Three days later the Kathi gentleman, accompanied by three of his nephews and all

---

[2] The Kathis are said to be descended from the Skuthoi or Scythians, They established themselves in Kathiawar in the 17th century and gave their name to the province.

splendidly mounted, arrived. Major Mulvaney offered them "kusumba," a mixture of opium and water, and they talked in Gujarati about the crops, the weather, Naja Wala's horses, about everything in fact except the object of the interview. Naja Wala, however, quite understood and after some twenty minutes he hinted to his nephews that the Major Sahib wished to speak to him about official business. Once they had gone Mulvaney said suddenly:

'Naja Wala, would you like to become an outlaw again?'

'No, Major Sahib, but I am quite willing to do so if the Government wish it.'

'Well, would you do me a favour and kidnap me and hold me to ransom?'

'After the Sahib's kindness to me about the Jornagar tax, I can refuse you nothing; but truly I do not understand. Why should I kidnap the Sahib? Moreover, I should soon be hunted down by the Agency police and you would be rescued without a ransom. But if the Sahib would explain, it would be better; for the Sahib is not like other topiwalas (Englishmen), he understands our people and talks our language.'

Major Mulvaney then proceeded to unbosom himself to his Kathi friend. He told him of his indebtedness and his vain struggle to pay off the Marwadi's debt and his intense desire to get out of India. This he could only fulfil if he could get the Government to pay a ransom of thirty thousand rupees, which they could share.

'But would it not do, Sahib, if I kidnapped the Marwadi and held him to ransom?'

'No indeed, Naja Wala, the Government would never pay thirty thousand rupees to free a Marwadi and the other Marwadis would soon get to the bottom of the matter.'

'Yes, Sahib,' said Naja Wala thoughtfully, "yours is a good plan and I would willingly earn fifteen thousand rupees myself so easily; but there is the Jornagar State. Their police would work with the Agency police and they would hunt us down.'

'That is true,' said Mulvaney, 'but we must promise to pay the Jornagar chief five thousand rupees out of the ransom. He is very hard up. That will still leave us twelve thousand five hundred each. I'll talk him over. Anyway, on Monday week I shall be riding in the Jornagar Gir with only one attendant and you must surround me with your men. I'll write a letter to the Government, telling them that I have been captured and that you want thirty thousand rupees and are threatening to cut off one of my ears if the ransom is not paid. I'll send this letter back by an attendant and I shall also stir up the Bombay newspaper. That will frighten the authorities.'

Naja Wala was delighted and after a last drink of 'kusumba' the two conspirators parted excellent friends.

The following Monday week about 4 p.m. Major Mulvaney, who had gone on a tour of inspection and was in tents not far away, rode with a mounted groom into the Gir forest that lay in Jornagar territory. When he reached an open glade, he pulled up his horse and waited; for this was the meeting place agreed on with Naja Wala. Some ten minutes later Naja Wala, with some ten or twelve retainers, rode up. They pointed guns at Mulvaney and ordered him and his groom to dismount. They seized the two horses and Naja Wala told the political officer that he would be a prisoner until his government ransomed him for thirty thousand rupees. This comedy was enacted for the benefit of the groom, to whom his master entrusted two letters, one addressed to the secretary of the Government and one to the editor of the *Bombay Gazette*. Once the groom was out of sight, the farce was dropped and Naja Wala became Mulvaney's attentive host.

'We shall have to ride, Major Sahib, another four or five miles into the Gir. I trust Your Honour is not fatigued. In any case a glass of kusumba will revive you.'

After the two had drunk off their opium and water, the Kathi and the Englishman rode into the forest for an hour and then dismounted. They had reached their halting place. The camping arrangements were primitive, but there was a cot under a tree for the prisoner and a country mattress and a blanket lay on it. Mulvaney could sleep anywhere, so he did not mind. He enjoyed the evening spent by the firelight and the general conversation in Gujarati which he followed quite easily. About ten p.m. Mulvaney went to his cot, put his saddle on it for a pillow and picketed his horse close by. The Kathis had no bedding and slept by their horses. The latter realised that their duty was to watch while their masters slept. They stood by the men, wide awake for some four hours, their bridles fastened to their sleeping owners wrists. At the end of the watch they whinnied, the men woke up and watched for a similar period, while the horses lay down. Then once more the men rested and the horses took the watch until dawn.

A week passed, then two weeks and no answer came from the Government. Naja Wala said gloomily: 'Well, Major Sahib, what are we to do? The Governor Sahib is perhaps waiting for us to send your ear.'

This was a kind of talk that was very unpleasing to Mulvaney; for although he was as brave as another, he was imaginative; and when he pictured Naja Wala sawing off his ear with a blunt sword, he felt quite faint.

'Ah now, Naja Wala, don't be in a hurry! The Governor is

a kind man, God bless him! And he would not like me to lose an ear. He'll be sending the money along one of these days.'

'Maybe, Sahib,' said the Kathi, "But we cannot stay here. We must move deeper still into the Gir, otherwise the Agency police will track us down in spite of the goodwill of the Jornagar chief.'

'Very well, let's move now," said Mulvaney. "I'm getting tired of this spot.'

They struck camp that evening and halted just on the boundary of Jornagar. They dared go no farther, for had they crossed it, the neighbouring State would have shewn them no mercy.

The Kathis went to sleep as usual with their horses watching by their masters' sides, when suddenly there was a terrific roar. Mulvaney sprang off his cot and saw the Kathis rushing about and firing recklessly into the undergrowth. Naja Wala was away for a few minutes and then came back with a dead man across his shoulder. He laid the body on the ground and covered its face with a shawl. He explained to Mulvaney that a lion had unexpectedly rushed the camp-there are still a few lions in the Kathiawar forests—and tried to seize one of the horses. The horse had dragged its master some way and then broken its reins. The lion, baulked of its prey, had killed the man and tried to carry him off, but frightened at the firing had dropped him. Mulvaney expressed his grief, but Naja Wala said indifferently: "He was a Bashio, one of my hereditary servants, and of no consequence.'

Mulvaney went to sleep again but about four a.m, he was again awakened. Naja Wala was standing by his cot.

'It's all right, Major Sahib, fear no more for your ears. I have cut off both those of that Bashio and we'll send the right ear at once to the Government in a registered packet and you will, no doubt, write a letter to go with it.'

Mulvaney felt immensely relieved and his ears tingled with pleasure.

'It was indeed God who sent that lion, Naja Wala.'

'Yes indeed,' replied the Kathi piously: 'without doubt God sent it so that the Sahib might keep both his ears. The Sahib would not have liked losing them.'

'You never said a truer word, Naja Wala,' said Mulvaney heartily.

The letter was written and the right ear placed carefully in a sealed envelope and so they reached the table of the Honourable Mr George Masséna Robinson, C.S.I., as I have already described. A day or two later the Political Agent got the telegram and forwarded it to Naja Wala through the Jornagar State. But Mulvaney refused to be released until half the money had been paid, so that he might have his passage money anyway. Rupees fifteen thousand were handed over to Naja Wala's agent in Jornagar and Mulvaney, with one side of his head heavily bandaged, returned to Jetalsar. There he received a letter from His Excellency's private secretary informing him that he could expect no further promotion. He at once applied for leave. This he got without difficulty and in a short while Naja Wala's agent received the remaining fifteen thousand. Out of this sum five thousand were paid to the Jornagar chief and the captive and his captor divided the rest, to their great satisfaction.

Once Major Mulvaney had got his leave and his passage money, it might have seemed that his difficulties were over; but they were not. Directly the Marwadi bankers saw that their debtor had been granted leave, they obtained a warrant for his arrest before judgment, so as to force him to give them security before he left India for the repayment of his loan. Mulvaney, however, got the editor of the *Bombay Gazette* first to publish that he was leaving by the P. and O. from Bombay and then later that he was embarking at Calcutta and going home via Japan. In the meantime he bought through his agents, Messrs. Wm. Watson & Co., a ticket by the Hall Line from Karachi very secretly and under a false name. Then he went by rail and embarked there. In the meantime the Marwadis had posted agents with warrants both at Bombay and at Calcutta. At the last moment the Marwadis got on their debtor's track and one of them climbed on board just as the steamer was weighing its anchor. He flourished his warrant, but in the passenger list there was no Major Mulvaney and it was impossible to recognise the fugitive debtor in the tall flaxen-haired quarter-master on deck. He looked more like a Viking than a political officer, wearing, as he did, a blond wig and a huge beard, specially provided by Messrs. Wm. Watson & Co. for just such cases. While the Marwadi was still searching, the ship got under way and he had to jump into the sea to get back to his boat. He sent a telegram to Aden, but the Hall Line boats did not call there, so Major Mulvaney got safely away and never paid the Marwadi bankers another farthing.

About a month or so after his escape, the Jornagar chief reported that his police had surprised Naja Wala and his gang and had killed them all. The Agency police, therefore, gave up their pursuit of the outlaws. Major Mulvaney read the news with genuine regret and sent a letter from Ireland to Naja Wala's son expressing his grief at the loss of his greatly esteemed friend.

Two years later Major Mulvaney sat in Mulvaney Castle. He was its owner, having inherited it from his brother Thaddeus, who had been killed in the hunting field six months after his younger brother's return. On the strength of his inheritance the Major had married Miss Norah O'Brien, the daughter of a successful Dublin engineer, with £5,000 of her own. She was very glad to become the chatelaine of Mulvaney Castle and he was only too pleased to use her money in restoring the castle and in rebuilding his tenants' cottages that had fallen into a dreadful state of disrepair. That morning the Major had found on his plate an Indian letter. He opened it and in a great state of excitement shouted across the table to his wife:

'Why it's from that old devil Naja Wala, who has been dead nearly two years.'

'Faith! it's the first time I've ever heard of a post from Hell!' said his wife, for like most Irish ladies she believed that the souls of non-Christians were dispatched to the infernal regions as a mere matter of routine.

'Ah, stop your talk, Norah, and just listen to what the ould blaygard says,' cried Mulvaney, his brogue coming out strongly in his excitement.

The letter read as if it had been first written in Gujarati and then laboriously translated into English.

'From the fortunate seaport of Bombay, Naja Wala, Kathi sends to Major Mulavaney Sahib greetings:

'From your honoured letter to my son, it seems that you have heard how I was shot by the Jornagar police. That was all a show to save me from the Agency police, who were following me. I escaped without hurt and came by steamer to Bombay, where by Your Honour's favour and my share of the money I have set up as a moneylender. Taught by Your Honour, I am making advances to young Englishmen, but never at a higher interest than they can afford. So they always repay me both capital and interest. The Marwadis are angry with me because I am taking away their business. Still what can they do? If a dog bark at an elephant, why should the elephant fear?

'My son is enjoying my estate in Jornagar, which he inherited at my death.

'I trust that Your Honour keeps good health and often feels Your Honour's ears, being glad that they are there.

With salaams,

Naja Wala.'

'Well, Patrick, I can't make head or tail of it,' commented Norah, who was unacquainted with Naja Wala's and her husband's diabolical conspiracy 'and what's all that rubbish about feeling your cars? They might be a wee ass's from the way he talks of them.'

Major Mulvaney, however, was not to be drawn; he said: 'I hope Naja Wala is not too confident. The Marwadis will certainly have him murdered if they can.'

Little Mrs Mulvaney could contain herself no longer: 'And why not indeed, if he is after writing them the stupid letters that he writes to you.' With this outburst she flounced out of the dining room to interview Biddy the cook.

The Marwadis did not murder Naja Wala, but Mulvaney was right to this extent: they did try hard to do it. Big business in India is just as unscrupulous as in Chicago. They bribed a band of Maratha dacoits to raid his house, kill him and plunder his property. But to kill a Kathi reiver, even when in retirement, is no light task as the hired brigands found. With a terrific sword cut Naja Wala slashed off one robber's arm. One of his nephews drove a silver-hilted dagger into another robber's heart. A second nephew struck with a mace a third ruffian so hard on the head that he dropped unconscious. The rest of the dacoits ran away. The police were sent for. The man with the dagger thrust and the one who had lost an arm died without regaining consciousness. But the third man recovered and told the police the whole story and gave them the names of the Marwadis who had hired the gang. It was a terrible shock for the Marwadis. It cost them at least ten thousand rupees, skilfully distributed among the lower ranks of the police, to stop a prosecution and they thereafter left Naja Wala alone: So he was not murdered, but as the French say he died de sa belle mort; in other words he died a natural death, certainly hastened by enormous draughts of opium and water, that became more and more frequent as his moneylending business prospered.

And what happened to Major Mulvaney? I expect he is still alive; at any rate I have never heard of his death. He must be well over ninety now, but that is nothing in the Irish Free State, where, if the register of Old Age Pensions is to be believed, no recipient of one ever dies before he has rounded off his hundred.

Money

By Richard Armour

Workers earn it,
Spendthrifts burn it,
Bankers lend it,
Women spend it,
Forgers fake it,
Taxes take it,
Dying leave it,
Heirs receive it,
Thrifty save it,
Misers crave it,
Robbers seize it,
Rich increase it,
Gamblers lose it...
I could use it!

Cricket at Dingley Dell

By Charles Dickens

The wickets were pitched, and so were a couple of marquees for the rest and refreshment of the contending parties. The game had not yet commenced. Two or three Dingley Dellers, and All-Muggletonians, were amusing themselves with a majestic air by throwing the ball carelessly from hand to hand; and several other gentlemen dressed like them, in straw hats, flannel jackets, and white trousers—a costume in which they looked very much like amateur stone-masons—were sprinkled about the tents, towards one of which Mr Wardle conducted the party.

Several dozen of How-are-you's?' hailed the old gentleman's arrival; and a general raising of the straw hats, and bending forward of the flannel jackets, followed his introduction of his guests as gentlemen from London, who were extremely anxious to witness the proceedings of the day, with which, he had no doubt, they would be greatly delighted

'You had better step into the marquee, I think, sir,' said one very stout gentleman, whose body and legs looked like half a gigantic roll of flannel, elevated on a couple of inflated pillow-cases.

'You'll find it much pleasanter, sir,' urged another stout

gentleman, who strongly resembled the other half of the roll of flannel aforesaid.

'You're very good,' said Mr Pickwick.

'This way,' said the first speaker; 'they notch in here—it's the best place in the whole field;' and the cricketer, panting on before, preceded them to the tent.

'Capital game—Smart sport—fine exercise-very,' were the words which fell upon Mr Pickwick's ear as he entered the tent; and the first object that met his eyes was his green-coated friend of the Rochester coach, holding forth, to the no small delight and edification of a select circle of the chosen of All-Muggleton. His dress was slightly improved, and he wore boots; but there was no mistaking him.

The stranger recognised his friends immediately; and, darting forward and seizing Mr Pickwick by the hand, dragged him to a seat with his usual impetuosity, talking all the while as if the whole of the arrangements were under his especial patronage and direction.

'This way—this way capital fun—lots of beer-hogsheads; rounds of beef—bullocks; mustard—cart-loads; glorious day. down with you make yourself at home-glad to see you—very.

Mr Pickwick sat down as he was bid, and Mr Winkle and Mr Snodgrass also complied with the directions of their mysterious friend. Mr Wardle looked on in silent wonder.

'Mr Wardle—a friend of mine,' said Mr Pickwick.

'Friend of yours!—My dear sir, how are you?—Friend of my friend's—give me your hand, sir—and the stranger grasped Mr Wardle's hand with all the fervour of a close intimacy of many years, and then stepped back a pace or two as if to take a full survey of his face and figure, and then shook hands with him again, if possible, more warmly than before.

'Well; and how came you here' said Mr Pickwick, with a smile in which benevolence struggled with surprise.

'Come,' replied the stranger-stopping at Crown-Crown at Muggleton—met a party—flannel jackets—White trousers—anchovy sandwiches—devilled kidneys—splendid fellows—glorious.'

Mr Pickwick was sufficiently versed in the stranger's system of stenography to infer from this rapid and disjointed communication that he had, somehow or other, contracted an acquaintance with the All-Muggletons, which he had converted, by a process peculiar to himself, into that extent of good-fellowship on which a general invitation may be easily founded. His curiosity was therefore satisfied, and putting on his spectacles he prepared himself to watch the play which was just commencing.

All-Muggleton had the first innings; and the interest became intense when Mr Dumkins and Mr Podder, two of the most renowned members of that most distinguished club, walked, bat in hand, to their respective wickets. Mr Luffey, the highest ornament of Dingley Dell, was pitched to bowl against the redoubtable Dumkins, and Mr Struggles was selected to do the same kind office for the hitherto unconquered Podder. Several players were stationed, to 'look out,' in different parts of the field, and each fixed himself into the proper attitude by placing one hand on each knee, and stooping very much as if he were 'making a back' for some beginner at leap-frog. All the regular players do this sort of thing—indeed it is generally supposed that it is quite impossible to look out properly in any other position.

The umpires were stationed behind the wickets; the scorers were prepared to notch the runs; a breathless silence ensued. Mr Luffey retired a few paces behind the wicket of the passive

Podder, and applied the ball to his right eye for several seconds. Dumkins confidently awaited its coming with his eyes fixed on the motions of Luffey.

'Play! suddenly cried the bowler. The ball flew from his hand straight and swift towards the centre stump of the wicket. The wary Dumkins was on the alert: it fell upon the tip of the bat, and bounded far away over the heads of the scouts, who had just stooped low enough to let it fly over them.

'Run—run—another. Now, then, throw her up—up with her—step there—another—no—yes—no—throw her up, throw her up!—Such were the shouts which followed the stroke; and at the conclusion of which All-Muggleton had scored two. Nor was Podder behindhand in earning laurels wherewith to garnish himself and Muggleton. He blocked the doubtful balls, missed the bad ones, took the good ones, and sent them flying to all parts of the field. The scouts were hot and tired; the bowlers were changed and bowled till their arms ached; but Dumkins and Podder remained unconquered. Did an elderly gentleman essay to stop the progress of the ball, it rolled between his legs or slipped between his fingers. Did a slim gentleman try to catch it, it struck him on the nose, and bounded pleasantly off with redoubled violence, while the slim gentleman's eyes filled with water, and his form writhed with anguish. Was it thrown straight up to the wicket, Dumkins had reached it before the ball. In short, when Dumkins was caught out, and Podder stumped out, All-Muggleton had notched some fifty-four, while the score of the Dingley Dellers was as blank as their faces. The advantage was too great to be recovered. In vain did the eager Luffey, and the enthusiastic Struggles, do all that skill and experience could suggest, to retain the ground Dingley Dell had lost in the contest it was of no avail; and in an early period of the winning game Dingley Dell gave in, and allowed the superior prowess of All Muggleton.

The stranger, meanwhile, had been eating, drinking, and talking, without cessation. At every good stroke he expressed his satisfaction and approval of the player in a most condescending and patronising manner, which could not fail to have been highly gratifying to the party concerned; while at every bad attempt at a catch, and every failure to stop the ball, he launched his personal displeasure at the head of the devoted individual in such denunciations as—'Ah, ah!—'stupid'—'Now, butter-fingers'—'Muff'—'Humbug' and so forth; ejaculations which seemed to establish him in the opinion of all around, as a most excellent and undeniable judge of the whole art and mystery of the noble game of cricket.

'Capital game—well played—some strokes admirable,' said the stranger, as both sides crowded into the tent, at the conclusion of the game.

'You have played it, sir?' inquired Mr Wardle, who had been much amused by his loquacity.

'Played it! Think I have thousands of times—not here—West Indies—exciting thing—hot work—very.'

'It must be rather a warm pursuit in such a climate,' observed Mr Pickwick.

'Warm!—red-hot—scorching—glowing. Played a match once—single wicket—friend the colonel—Sir Thomas Blazo—who should get the greatest number of runs.—Won the toss first innings—seven o'clock A.M.—six natives to look out—went in; kept in—heat intense—natives all fainted—taken away—fresh half-dozen ordered—fainted also—Blazo bowling—supported by two natives—couldn't bowl me out—fainted too—cleared away the colonel—wouldn't give in—fainted too—cleared away the colonel—wouldn't give in—faithful attendant—Quanko Samba last man left—sun so hot, bat in blisters, ball scorched brown—five hundred and seventy runs, rather exhausted—Quanko mustered up last remaining strength—bowled me out—had a bath, and went out to dinner.'

And what became of what's-his-name, sir?' inquired an old gentleman.

'Blazo?'

No—the other gentleman.'

'Quanko Samba?'

'Yes, sir.'

'Poor Quanko—never recovered it—bowled on, on my account—bowled off, on his own—died, sir.' Here the stranger buried his countenance in a brown jug, but whether to hide his emotion or imbibe its contents, we cannot distinctly affirm. We only know that he paused suddenly, drew a long and deep breath, and looked anxiously on, as two of the principal members of the Dingley Dell club approached Mr Pickwick, and said—

'We are about to partake of a plain dinner at the Blue Lion, sir; we hope you and your friends will join us.'

'Of course,' said Mr Wardle, among our friends we include Mr—;' and he looked towards the stranger.

'Jingle,' said that versatile gentleman, taking the hint at once. 'Jingle—Alfred Jingle, Esq., of No Hall, Nowhere.'

'I shall be very happy, I am sure,' said Mr Pickwick.

'So shall I,' said Mr Alfred Jingle, drawing one arm through Mr Pickwick's, and another through Mr Wardle's, as he whispered confidentially in the ear of the former gentleman—

'Devilish good dinner—cold, but capital—peeped into the room this morning—fowls and pies, and all that sort of thing—pleasant fellows these well behaved, too—very.'

There being no further preliminaries to arrange, the company straggled into the town in little knots of twos and threes; and within a quarter of an hour were all seated in the great room of the Blue Lion Inn, Muggleton—Mr Dumkins acting as chairman, and Mr Luffey officiating as vice.

There was a vast deal of talking and rattling of knives and forks, and plates; a great running about of three ponderous headed waiters, and a rapid disappearance of the substantial viands on the table; to each and every of which item of confusion, the facetious Mr Jingle lent the aid of half a dozen ordinary men at least. When everybody had eaten as much as possible, the cloth was removed, bottles, glasses, and dessert were placed on the table; and the waiters withdrew to 'clear away' or in other words, to appropriate to their own private use and emolument whatever remnants of the eatables and drinkables they could contrive to lay their hands on.

From *The Pickwick Papers,* 1837

Cricket—Field Placings

Long leg has a cramp in one leg,
Short leg has a cramp in two;
Twelfth man is fielding at mid-off,
Because mid-on's gone off to the loo.
As short square leg has a long leg,
Long-off has been moved further off;
Silly-point goes back to gully
Cover-point backs off a pace or two.
Everyone is thinking of the drinks' trolley
When first slip lets a catch through his fingers,
Forgetting the old ball is now new.

The Cricket Match

By A.G. Macdonnel

'Don't forget Saturday morning Charing Cross Underground Station, ran the telegram which arrived at Royal Avenue during the week, 'at ten-fifteen sharp whatever you do don't be late.—Hodge.'

Saturday morning was bright and sunny, and at ten minutes past ten Donald Cameron arrived at the Embankment entrance of Charing Cross Underground Station, carrying a small suitcase full of clothes suitable for outdoor sports and pastimes. He was glad that he had arrived too early, for it would have been a dreadful thing for a stranger and a foreigner to have kept such a distinguished man, and his presumably distinguished colleagues, even for an instant from their national game. Laying his bag down on the pavement and putting one foot upon it carefully for Donald had heard stories of the surpassing dexterity of metropolitan thieves, he waited eagerly for the hands of a neighbouring clock to mark the quarter-past. At twenty minutes to eleven an effeminate-looking young man, carrying a cricketing bag and wearing a pale-blue silk jumper up to his ears, sauntered up, remarked casually, 'You playing?' and, on receiving an answer in the affirmative, dumped his bag at Donald's feet and said, 'Keep an eye on that, like a good fellow. I'm going to get a shave,' and sauntered off round the corner.

At five minutes to eleven there was a respectable muster, six of the team having assembled. But at five minutes past a disintegrating element was introduced by the arrival of Mr Harcourt with the news, which he announced with the air of a shipwrecked mariner who has, after twenty-five years of vigilance, seen a sail, that in the neighbourhood of Charing Cross the pubs opened at 11 a.m. So that when Mr Hodge himself turned up at twenty-five minutes past eleven, resplendent in flannels, a red-and-white football shirt with a lace-up collar, and a blazer of purple-and-yellow stripes, each stripe being at least two inches across, and surmounted by a purple-and-yellow cap that made him somehow reminiscent of one of the Michelin twins, if not both, he was justly indignant at the slackness of his team,

'They've no sense of time,' he told Donald repeatedly. "We're late as it is. The match is due to begin at half past eleven, and it's fifty miles from here. I should have been here myself two hours ago, but I had my Sunday article to do. It really is too bad.'

When the team, now numbering nine men, had been extricated from the tavern and had been marshalled on the pavement, counted, recounted, and the missing pair identified, it was pointed out by the casual youth who had returned shining and pomaded from the barber, that the charabanc had not yet arrived.

Mr Hodge's indignation became positively alarming and he covered twenty yards to the public telephone box almost as quickly as Mr Harcourt covered the forty yards back to the door of the pub. Donald remained on the pavement to guard the heap of suitcases, cricket-bags, and stray equipment—one player had arrived with a pair of flannels rolled in a tight ball under his arm and a left-hand batting glove, while another had contributed a cardboard box which he had bought at Hamley's on the way down, and which contained six composite cricket-balls, boys' size, and a pair of bails. It was just as well that Donald did remain on guard, partly because no-one else seemed to care whether the luggage was stolen or not, partly because Mr Hodge emerged in a perfect frenzy a minute or two later from the telephone box to borrow two pennies to put in the slot, and partly because by the time the telephone call was at last in full swing and Mr Hodge's command over the byways of British invective was enjoying complete freedom of action, the charabanc rolled up beside the kerb.

At 12.30 it was decided not to wait for the missing pair, and the nine cricketers started off. At 2.30, after halts at Catford, the 'White Hart' at Sevenoaks, the 'Angel' at Tunbridge Wells, and three smaller inns at tiny villages, the charabanc drew up triumphantly beside the cricket ground of the Kentish village of Fordenden....

At twenty minutes to three, Mr Hodge had completed his rather tricky negotiations with the Fordenden captain, and had arranged that two substitutes should be lent by Fordenden in order that the visitors should field eleven men, and that nine men on each side should bat. But just as the two men on the Fordenden side, who had been detailed for the unpleasant duty of fielding for both sides and batting for neither, had gone off home in high dudgeon, a motor-car arrived containing not only Mr Hodge's two defaulters, but a third gentleman in flannels as well, who swore stoutly that he had been invited by Mr Hodge to play and affirmed that he was jolly well going to play. Whoever stood down, it wasn't going to be him. Negotiations therefore had to be reopened, the pair of local Achilles had to be recalled, and at ten minutes to three the match began upon a twelve-a-side basis.

Mr Hodge, having won the toss by a system of his own founded upon the differential calculus and the Copernican theory, sent in his opening pair to bat. One was James Livingstone, a very sound club cricketer, and the other one was called, simply, Boone. Boone was a huge, awe-inspiring colossus of a man, weighing at least eighteen stone and wearing all the majestic trapping of a Cambridge Blue. Donald felt that it was hardly fair to loose such cracks upon a humble English village until he fortunately remembered that he, of all people, a foreigner, admitted by courtesy to the National Game, ought not to set himself up to be a judge of what is, and what is not, cricket.

The Fordenden team ranged themselves at the bidding of their captain, the Fordenden baker, in various spots of vantage amid the daisies, buttercups, dandelions, vetches, thistle-down, and clumps of dark-red sorrel; and the blacksmith having taken in, just for luck as it were, yet another reef in his snake-buckle belt, prepared to open the attack. It so happened that, at the end at which he was to bowl, the ground behind the wicket was level for a few yards and then sloped away rather abruptly, so that it was only during the last three or four intensive, galvanic yards of his run that the blacksmith, who took a long run, was visible to the batsman or indeed to anyone on the field of play except the man stationed in the deep field behind him. This man saw nothing of the game except the blacksmith walking back dourly and the blacksmith running up ferociously, and occasionally a ball driven smartly over the brow of the hill in his direction.

The sound club player having taken guard, having twiddled

his bat round several times in a nonchalant manner, and having stared arrogantly at each fieldsman in turn, was somewhat surprised to find that, although the field was ready, no bowler was visible. His doubts, however, were resolved a second or two later, when the blacksmith came up, breasting the slope superbly like a mettlesome combination of Vulcan and Venus Anadyomene. The first ball which he delivered was a high full-pitch to leg, of appalling velocity. It must have lighted upon a bare patch among the long grass near long-leg, for it rocketed, first bounce into the hedge, and four byes were reluctantly signalled by the village umpire. The row of gaffers on the rustic bench shook their heads, agreed that it was many years since four byes had been signalled on that ground, and called for more pints of old-and-mild. The other members of Mr Hodge's team blanched visibly and called for more pints of bitter. The youngish professor of ballistics, who was in next, muttered something about muzzle velocities and started to do a sum on the back of an envelope.

The second ball went full-pitch into the wicket-keeper's stomach and there was a delay while the deputy wicket-keeper was invested with the pads and gloves of office. The third ball, making a noise like a partridge, would have hummed past Mr Livingstone's left ear had he not dexterously struck it out of the ground for six, and the fourth took his leg bail with a bullet-like full-pitch. Ten runs for one wicket, last man six. The professor got the fifth ball on the left ear and went back to the 'Three Horseshoes', while Mr Harcourt had the singular misfortune to hit his wicker before the sixth ball was even delivered. Ten runs for two wickets and one man retired hurt. A slow left-hand bowler was on at the other end, the local rate-collector, a man whose whole life was one of infinite patience and guile. Off his first ball the massive Cambridge Blue was easily stumped, having executed a movement that aroused the professional admiration of the Ancient who was leaning upon his scythe. Donald was puzzled that so famous a player should play so execrable a stroke until it transpired, later on, that a wrong impression had been created and that the portentous Boone had gained his Blue at Cambridge for rowing and not for cricket. Ten runs for three wickets and one man hurt.

The next player was a singular young man. He was small and quiet, and he wore perfectly creased white flannels, white silk socks, a pale-pink silk shirt and a white cap. On the way down in the charabanc he had taken little part in the conversation and even less in the beer-drinking. There was a retiring modesty about him that made him conspicuous in that cricket eleven, and there was a gentleness, an almost finicky gentleness, about his movements which hardly seemed virile and athletic. He looked as if a fast ball would knock the bat out of his hands. Donald asked someone what his name was, and was astonished to learn that he was the famous novelist, Robert Southcott, himself.

Just as this celebrity, holding his bat as delicately as if it was a flute or a fan, was picking his way through the daisies and thistle-down towards the wicket, Mr Hodge rushed anxiously, tankard in hand, from the 'Three Horseshoes' and bellowed in a most unpoetical voice: 'Play carefully, Bobby. Keep your end up. Runs don't matter.'

'Very well, Bill,' replied Mr Southcott sedately. Donald was interested by this little exchange. It was the Team Spirit at work—the captain instructing his man to play a type of game that was demanded by the state of the team's fortunes, and the individual loyally suppressing his instincts to play a different type of game.

Mr Southcott took guard modestly, glanced furtively round

the field as if it was an impertinence to suggest that he would survive long enough to make a study of the fieldsmen's positions worth while, and hit the rate-collector's first ball over the 'Three Horseshoes' into a hayfield. The ball was retrieved by a mob of screaming urchins, handed back to the rate-collector, who scratched his head and then bowled his fast yorker, which Mr Southcott hit into the saloon bar of the 'Shoes', giving Mr Harcourt such a fright that he required several pints before he fully recovered his nerve. The next ball was very slow and crafty, endowed as it was with every iota of finger-spin and brain-power which a long-service rate-collector could muster. In addition, it was delivered at the extreme end of the crease so as to secure a background of dark laurels instead of a dazzling white screen, and it swung a little in the air; a few moments later the urchins, by this time delirious with ecstasy, were fishing it out of the squire's trout stream with a bamboo pole and an old bucket.

The rate-collector was bewildered. He had never known such a travesty of the game. It was not cricket. It was slogging; it was wild, unscientific bashing; and, furthermore, his reputation was in grave danger. The instalments would be harder than ever to collect, and Heaven knew they were hard enough to collect as it was, what with bad times and all. His three famous deliveries had been treated with contempt—the leg-break, the fast yorker, and the slow, swinging off-break out of the laurel bushes. What on earth was he to try now! Another six and he would be laughed out of the parish. Fortunately the village umpire came out of a trance of consternation to the rescue. Thirty-eight years of umpiring for the Fordenden Cricket Club had taught him a thing or two, and he called 'Over' firmly and marched off to square leg. The rate-collector was glad to give way to a Free Forester, who had been specially imported for this match. He was only a moderate bowler, but it was felt that it was worthwhile giving him a trial, if only for the sake of the scarf round his waist and his cap. At the other end, the fast bowler pounded away grimly until an unfortunate accident occurred. Mr Southcott had been treating with apologetic contempt those of his deliveries which came within reach, and the blacksmith's temper had been rising for some time. An urchin shouted, 'Take him off!' and the other urchins, for whom Mr Southcott was by now a firmly established deity, had screamed with delight. The captain had held one or two ominous consultations with the wicket-keeper and other advisers, and the blacksmith knew that his dismissal was at hand unless he produced a supreme effort.

It was the last ball of the over. He halted at the wicket before going back for his run, glared at Mr Harcourt, who had been driven out to umpire by his colleagues—greatly to the regret of Mr Bason, the landlord of the 'Shoes'—glared at Mr Southcott, took another reef in his belt, shook out another inch in his braces, spat on his hand, swung his arm three or four times in a meditative sort of way, grasped the ball tightly in his colossal palm, and then turned smartly about and marched off like a Pomeranian grenadier and vanished over the brow of the hill. Mr Southcott, during these proceedings, leant elegantly upon his bat and admired the view. At last, after a long stillness, the ground shook, the grasses waved violently, small birds arose with shrill clamours, a loud puffing sound alarmed the butterflies, and the blacksmith, looking more like Venus Anadyomene than ever, came thundering over the crest. The world held its breath. Among the spectators conversation was suddenly hushed. Even the urchins, understanding somehow that they were assisting at a crisis in affairs, were silent for a moment as the mighty figure swept up to the crease. It was the charge of Von Bredow's Dragoons at Gravelotte over again.

But alas for human ambitions! Mr Harcourt, swaying slightly from leg to leg, had understood the menacing glare of the bowler, had marked the preparation for a titanic effort, and—for he was not a poet for nothing—knew exactly what was going on. And Mr Harcourt sober had a very pleasant sense of humour, but Mr Harcourt rather drunk was a perfect demon of impishness. Sober, he occasionally resisted a temptation to try to be funny. Rather drunk, never. As the giant whirlwind of volcanic energy rushed past him to the crease, Mr Harcourt, quivering with excitement and internal laughter, and wobbling uncertainly upon his pins, took a deep breath and bellowed, 'No ball!'

It was too late for the unfortunate bowler to stop himself. The ball flew out of his hand like a bullet and hit third-slip, who was not looking, full pitch on the knee-cup. With a yell of agony third-slip began hopping about like a stork until he tripped over a tussock of grass and fell on his face in a bed of nettles, from which he sprang up again with another drum-splitting yell. The blacksmith himself was flung forward by his own irresistible momentum, startled out of his wits by Mr Harcourt's bellow in his ear, and thrown off his balance by his desperate effort to prevent himself from delivering the ball, and the result was that his gigantic feet got mixed up among each other and he fell heavily in the centre of the wicket, knocking up a cloud of dust and dandelion-seed and twisting his ankle. Rooks by hundreds arose in protest from the vicarage cedars. The urchins howled like intoxicated banshees. The gaffers gaped. Mr Southcott gazed modestly at the ground. Mr Harcourt gazed at the heavens, Mr Harcourt did not think the world had ever been, or could ever be again, quite such a capital place, even though he had laughed internally so much that he had got hiccups.

Mr Hodge, emerging at that moment from the 'Three Horseshoes', surveyed the scene and then the scoreboard with an imperial air. Then he roared in the same rustic voice as before: 'You needn't play safe any more, Bob. Play your own game.' 'Thank you, Bill,' replied Mr Southcott, as sedately as ever, and, on the resumption of the game, he fell into a kind of cricketing trance, defending his wicket skilfully from straight balls, ignoring crooked ones, and scoring one more run in a quarter of an hour before he inadvertently allowed, for the first time during his innings, a ball to strike his person.

'Out!' shrieked the venerable umpire, before anyone had time to appeal.

The score at this point was sixty-nine for six, last man fifty-two.

Major Canamus

By A.G. Shirreff

I

Have I told you (said the Major)
How I nearly once collided
With a camel? Few, I wager,
Would have come off clean as I did.

I was on my motor cycle,
Doing eighty miles an hour—
It's astounding what that bike'll
Do with only three horse power.

One of those canal hog-backs I'd
Cleared—their gradients are a scandal—
When I saw a camel's backside
Rising straight above my handle.

Well, you know how camels straddle.
I was quite prepared. The fact is
Standing on a moving saddle.
Is a trick I often practise.

Up I sprang, exactly clearing
Rump and hump and neck and crest of him.
And the bike went on careering
Through his legs beneath the rest of him.

My descent was timed precisely
With the bicycle's emerging,
And I hit the saddle nicely,
Not a finger's breadth diverging.

Not so dusty (said the Major)
For a first attempt at flying.
Some of you young bloods, I wager,
Would have found it rather trying.

II

I was never known to miss a
Tiger (said the Major), never.
Once I lost one in Orissa.
That was sheer bad luck, however.

I, you see, was dry fly fishing
On the lower Mahanadi,
Having decent sport, but wishing
That the banks were not so muddy.

I was whisking all my slack round—
Fifty yards—(I'm fairly apt at it)—
When a tiger in the back-ground
Must have seen my fly and snapped at it.

Rising with the fly and soaring
Over me into the river

Shot a monstrous brute, whose roaring
Made the very mud-banks quiver.

'Twas a bigger fish than ever
Fisherman has filled his creel with.
One that needed fairly clever
Handling, you'll admit, to deal with.

I had nearly got him landed
After twenty minutes' tussle.
'Twas an effort that demanded
All my powers of mind and muscle.

Under us the mud was quaking.
When the tug was nearly over, he
Slipped and fell, my tackle breaking;
Sank this time beyond recovery.

With a gaff my sole protection
It was just as well, it may be.
So I think on cool reflection,
But I cried then like a baby.

III

Danger? Said the Major. What of it?
I have had my share of dangers.
In the hottest of the hot of it
Fear and I have still been strangers.

When by my shikari's bungle
I was left alone benighted
In a truly howling jungle,
Was I in the least excited!

No, Sir. Though there might have been a
Tiger through the forest ranging
Or a supperless hyena,
My composure was unchanging.

Left without a light or weapon,
I was situated so as
Stirring to be sure to step on
Sleeping porcupines or boas.

On the level any paltry
Panther could surprise and floor me:
So I climbed the nearest sal tree
To the highest branch that bore me.

And, though every limb was aching,
Resolutely I sat there, Sir,
Sat until the dawn was breaking,
Making noises like a bear, Sir.

You may smile, but while I did it
I Didn't find it so divertin'.
Savoir faire and intrepidity
Saved my life that night for certain.

IV

That's a splendid head of ibex,
My collection's finest feature,
Said the Major. I'll describe exactly
How I bagged the creature.

I was on a mountain brow, Sir,
In Ladakh, with my shikari,

And the double-barrelled Mauser
I invariably carry.

On an ibex when my eye fell
Fifteen thousand feet beneath us, and
Just within range of my rifle,
Though it's sighted but to three thousand.

'Twas an awkward situation,
For I had to take, in order
To get in a shot, my station
On a precipice's border.

Head and trunk in space to dangle
Is a ticklish thing to do, Sir,
All the more so when the angle
Of your legs is one in two, Sir.

There I hung, and my shikari
Lay behind, my ankles gripping.
Just as I had fixed my quarry,
Zounds! I felt we both were slipping.

The position was appalling.
There was nothing that could hinder us,
Short of miracles, from falling
To the bottom, smashed to flinders.

But with instant resolution
And the sang-froid of a Briton,
I arrived at a solution
Everyone would not have hit on.

As I felt my ankles getting
Loose from my shikari's tether,
Bang! I pulled the triggers, letting
Both the barrels off together.

The concussion was tremendous,
For I had a double charge in,
And it just sufficed to send us
Back to safety on the margin.

And the ibex? Well, the trophy's
There to prove that I did kill it.
For my rifle did its office.
Both the bullets found their billet.

V

Now I'm getting an old stager,
Doctors recommend me walking;
For which reason (said the Major)
My chief exercise is stalking.
('Stalking,' Sir, I said,—not 'talking').

And, in stalking, past disputing,
My most curious experience
Was the one I had when shooting
Barasingh up North of Terhi once.

I had seen a fourteen-tiner
Standing clear on the horizon.
Antlers heavier or finer
I had never yet set eyes on.

I took aim, and hit it neatly
(As I thought) behind the shoulder.
Like a log it fell, completely
Hidden by a jutting boulder.

As I started to retrieve it,
At the height of my ambition,
Up it jumped, if you'll believe it,
In the very same position.

And I saw to my amazement
That both horns had one tine wanting,
Which—I knew my rifle's ways—meant
That I must have held it slanting.

Once again I aimed, and shot it
(As I thought) behind the shoulder.
Once again I must have got it,
For it fell behind the boulder.

But I lay and rubbed my eyes, Sir,
For again I must have missed. I'm
Jiggered if it didn't rise, Sir,
And with four tines missing this time.

Well, Sir, in succession eight—or
Rather seven times I downed it.
Seven times, a moment later,
Perched on the same rock I found it.

And it made its reappearance,
Still with antlers one tine shorter,
With such dogged perseverance
That I thought of giving quarter.

But by then its cup was full, it
Had no horns left to diminish,
And my eighth and final bullet
Brought the struggle to a finish.

Though it really scarcely mattered,
As the horns would be past praying for,
Irrecoverably scattered—
Still, I thought a look worth staying for.

But when I had made my way there,
Zounds! My riches were embarrassing,
For, instead of one, I found there
Seven buck and one doe barasingh.

There you are, Sir. That's the best of them.
As you see, instead of twelve, it
Has fourteen tines. All the rest of them
Were, I must confess, on velvet.

VI

Risky work, Sir, tiger-stalking,
Said the Major, monstrous risky.
(Thirsty weather this for talking
Thank you. Mine's another whisky).

Mirzapur, when I was sent there,
Stank of tiger; you could wind 'em
Almost anywhere you went there;
That's till I and W—thinned 'em.

Through the deep-cut nullahs creeping
I had tracked and killed a couple, and

The horizon now was sweeping
For another on the upland.

At my glasses' range extreme I
Searched each hillock, bush and boulder,
While my rifle hung, to free my
Hands, suspended from my shoulder.

Having nearly boxed the compass, I
Looked behind me, and, Great Cæsar!
I confess I gave a jump as I
Saw the tables turned on me, Sir.

Three feet off was a terrific
Tiger in the act of springing,
And my sole and sure specific
Useless at my back was swinging.

Oh, of course you guess the sequel—
Seeing me (he thought) receding
To the middle of next week, well
Over me the brute went speeding.

With a bullet in his occiput
He was greeted as he landed.
Coming here, I lost the box I put
His skin in—at least my man did!

First published in *The Pioneer*, Allahabad, 1917

George and Ranji

When I heard that my cousin George had again escaped from the mental hospital in a neighbouring town, I knew it wouldn't be long before he turned up at my doorstep. It usually happens at the approach of the cricket season. No problem, I thought. I'll just bundle him into a train and take him back to the hospital.

Cousin George had been there, off and on, for a few years. He wasn't the violent type and was given a certain amount of freedom with the result that he occasionally wandered off by himself, sometimes, to try and take in a Test match. You see, George did not suffer from the delusion that he was Napoleon or Ghengis Khan, he was convinced that he was the great Ranji, Prince of Cricketers, and that he had just been selected to captain India—quite forgetting that Ranji had actually played for England!

So when George turned up on my front steps I wasn't surprised to find him carrying a cricket bar in one hand and a protective box in the other.

'Aren't you ready?' he asked. 'The match starts at 11.'

'There's plenty of time.' I said, recalling that the train left at 11.15. 'Why don't you come in and relax while I get ready?'

George sat down and asked for a glass of beer. I brought him one and he promptly emptied it over a pot of ferns.

'They look thirsty,' he said. I dressed hurriedly, anxious to get moving before he started practising his latest cuts on my cutglass decanter. Then, arm in arm, we walked to the gate and hailed an auto rickshaw.

'Railway station,' I whispered to the driver.

'Ferozeshah Kotla,' said George in rising tones, naming Delhi's famous cricket ground. No matter. I thought, I'll straighten out the driver as we go along, I bundled George into the rickshaw and we were soon heading in the direction of the Kotla.

'Railway station,' I said again, in tones that could not be denied.

'Kotla,' said cousin George, just as firmly.

The scooter driver kept right on course for the cricket ground. Apparently George had made a better impression on him.

'Look,' I said, tapping the driver on the shoulder. "This is my cousin and he's not quite right in the head. He's just escaped from a mental asylum and if I'm to get him back there tonight, we must catch the 11.15 train.'

The scooter driver slowed down and looked from cousin George to me and back again. George gave him a winning smile and looking in my direction, tapped his forehead significantly. The driver nodded in sympathy and kept straight on for the Kotla.

◆

Well, I've always believed that the dividing line between sanity and insanity is a very thin one, but I had never realised it was quite so thin—too thin for my own comfort! Who was crazy, George, me or the driver?

We had almost reached the Kotla and I had no intention of watching over cousin George through a whole day's play. He gets excited at cricket matches—which is strange considering how dull they can be. On one occasion, he broke through the barriers and walked up to the wicket with his bat, determined to bat at No 3 (Ranji's favourite position, apparently) and assaulted an umpire who tried to escort him from the ground. On another occasion, he streaked across the ground, wearing nothing but his protective box.

But it was I who confirmed the driver's worst fears by jumping off the rickshaw as it slowed down, and making my getaway. I've never been able to discover if cousin George had any money with him, or if the rickshaw driver got paid. Rickshaw drivers are inclined at times to be violent, but then so are inmates of mental hospitals. Anyway, George seems to have no memory of the incident.

Three days later, I received word from the hospital that he had returned of his own accord, boasting that he had hit a century—so presumably, he had participated in the match in some form or another.

All's well that ends well, or so I like to think. Cousin George was not usually a violent man, but I have a funny feeling about the rickshaw driver. I never saw him again in Delhi, and unless he had moved elsewhere, I'm afraid his disappearance might well be connected with cousin George's rickshaw ride. After all, the Jamuna is very near the Kotla.

The Zigzag Walk

Uncle Ken always maintained that the best way to succeed in life was to zigzag. 'If you keep going off in new directions,' he declared, "you will meet new career opportunities!'

Well, opportunities certainly came Uncle Ken's way, but he was not a success in the sense that Dale Carnegie or Deepak Chopra would have defined a successful man...

In a long life devoted to 'muddling through' with the help of the family, Uncle Ken's many projects had included a chicken farm (rather like the one operated by Ukridge in Wodehouse's *Love Among the Chickens*) and a mineral water bottling project. For this latter enterprise, he bought a thousand old soda-water bottles and filled them with sulphur water from the springs five miles from Dehra. It was good stuff, taken in small quantities, but drunk one bottle at a time it proved corrosive—'sulphur and brimstone' as one irate customer described it—and angry buyers demonstrated in front of the house, throwing empty bottles over the wall into grandmother's garden.

Grandmother was furious—more with Uncle Ken than with the demonstrators and made him give everyone's money back.

'You have to be healthy and strong to take sulphur water,' he explained later.

'I thought it was supposed to make you healthy and strong,' I said.

Grandfather remarked that it did not compare with plain soda-water, which he took with his whisky. "Why don't you just bottle soda-water?' he said, 'there's a much bigger demand for it.'

But Uncle Ken believed that he had to be original in all things. 'The secret to success is to zigzag,' he said.

'You certainly zigzagged round the garden when your customers were throwing their bottles back at you,' said Grandmother.

Uncle Ken also invented the zigzag walk.

The only way you could really come to know a place well, was to walk in a truly haphazard way. To make a zigzag walk you take the first turning to the left, the first to the right, then the first to the left and so on. It can be quite fascinating provided you are in no hurry to reach your destination. The trouble was that Uncle Ken used this zigzag method even when he had a train to catch.

When Grandmother asked him to go to the station to meet Aunt Mabel and her children, who were arriving from Lucknow, he zigzagged through town, taking in the botanical gardens in the west and the limestone factories to the east, finally reaching the station by way of the goods yard, in order as he said, "to take it by surprise'.

Nobody was surprised, least of all Aunt Mabel who had taken a tonga and reached the house while Uncle Ken was still sitting on the station platform, waiting for the next train to come in. I was sent to fetch him.

'Let's zigzag home again,' he said.

'Only on one condition, we eat chaat every 15 minutes,' I said.

So we went home by way of all the most winding bazaars, and in north-Indian towns they do tend to zigzag, stopping at numerous chaat and halwai shops, until Uncle Ken had finished his money. We got home very late and were scolded by everyone; but as Uncle Ken told me, we were pioneers and had to expect to be misunderstood and even maligned. Posterity would recognise the true value of zigzagging.

'The zigzag way,' he said, 'is the diagonal between heart and reason.'

In our more troubled times, had he taken to preaching on the subject, he might have acquired a large following of dropouts. But Uncle Ken was the original dropout. He would have not tolerated others.

Had he been a space traveller he would have gone from star to star, zigzagging across the Milky Way.

Uncle Ken would not have succeeded in getting anywhere very fast, but I think he did succeed in getting at least one convert (myself) to see his point: 'When you zigzag, you are not choosing what to see in this world but you are giving the world a chance to see you!'

The Decline of the Drama

By *Stephen Leacock*

Coming up home the other night in my car (the Guy Street car), I heard a man who was hanging onto a strap say: 'The drama is just turning into a bunch of talk.' This set me thinking; and I was glad that it did, because I am being paid by this paper to think once a week, and it is wearing. Some days I never think from morning till night.

This decline of the drama is a thing on which I feel deeply and bitterly; for I am, or I have been, something of an actor myself. I have only been in amateur work, I admit, but still I have played some mighty interesting parts. I have acted in Shakespeare as a citizen, I have been a fairy in 'A Midsummer Night's Dream,' and I was once one end (choice of ends) of a camel in a pantomime. I have had other parts too, such as 'A Voice Speaks From Within,' or 'A Noise Is Heard Without,' or a 'Bell Rings From Behind,' and a lot of things like that. I played as A Noise for seven nights, before crowded houses where people were being turned away from the door, and I have been a Groan and a Sigh and a Tumult, and once I was a 'Vision Passes Before the Sleeper.'

So when I talk of acting and of the spirit of the Drama, I speak of what I know.

Naturally, too, I was brought into contact, very often into quite intimate personal contact, with some of the greatest actors of the day. I don't say it in any way of boasting, but merely because to those of us who love the stage all dramatic souvenirs are interesting. I remember, for example, that when Wilson Barrett played 'The Bar' and had to wear the queer suit with the scales, it was I who put the glue on him.

And I recall a conversation with Sir Henry Irving one night when he said to me, 'Fetch me a glass of water, will you?' and I said, 'Sir Henry, it is not only a pleasure to get it but it is to me, as a humble devotee of the art that you have ennobled, a high privilege. I will go further' 'Do,' he said. Henry was like that, quick, sympathetic, what we call in French 'vibrant.'

Forbes Robertson I shall never forget: he owes me 50 cents. And as for Martin Harvey—I simply cannot call him Sir John, we are such dear old friends—he never comes to this town without at once calling in my services to lend a hand in his production. No doubt everybody knows that splendid play in which he appears, called 'The Breed of the Treshams.'

There is a torture scene in it, a most gruesome thing. Harvey, as the hero, has to be tortured, not on the stage itself, but off the stage in a little room at the side. You can hear him howling as he is tortured. Well, it was I who was torturing him. We are so used to working together that Harvey didn't want to let anybody do it but me.

So naturally I am a keen friend and student of the Drama: and I hate to think of it going all to pieces.

The trouble with it is that it is becoming a mere mass of conversation and reflection: nothing happens in it; the action is all going out of it and there is nothing left but thought. When actors begin to think, it is time for a change. They are not fitted for it.

Now in my day—I mean when I was at the apogee of my reputation (I think that is the word—it may be apologee—I forget)—things were very different. What we wanted was action—striking, climatic, catastrophic action, in which things not only happened, but happened suddenly and all in a lump.

And we always took care that the action happened in some place that was worth while, not simply in an ordinary room with ordinary furniture, the way it is in the new drama. The scene was laid in a lighthouse (top story), or in a mad house (at midnight), or in a power house, or a dog house, or a bath house, in short, in some place with a distinct local color and atmosphere.

I remember in the case of the first play I ever wrote (I write plays, too) the manager to whom I submitted it asked me at once, the moment he glanced at it, 'Where is the action of this laid?' 'It is laid,' I answered, 'in the main sewer of a great city.' 'Good, good,' he said; 'keep it there.'

In the case of another play the manager said to me, 'What are you doing for atmosphere?' 'The opening act,' I said, 'is in a steam laundry.' 'Very good,' he answered as he turned over the pages, 'and have you brought in a condemned cell?' I told him that I had not. 'That's rather unfortunate,' he said, 'because we are especially anxious to bring in a condemned cell. Three of the big theaters have got them this season, and I think we ought to have it in. Can you do it?' 'Yes,' I said, 'I can, if it's wanted. PU look through the cast, and no doubt I can find one at least of them that ought to be put to death.' 'Yes, Yes,' said the manager enthusiastically, 'I am sure you can.'

But I think of all the settings that we used, the lighthouse plays were the best. There is something about a lighthouse that you don't get in a modern drawing room. What it is, I don't know; but there's a difference. I always have liked a lighthouse play, and never have enjoyed acting so much, have never thrown myself into acting so deeply, as in a play of that sort.

There is something about a lighthouse—the way you see it in the earlier scenes—with the lantern shining out over the black waters that suggests security, fidelity, faithfulness, to a trust. The stage used generally to be dim in the first part of a lighthouse play, and you could see the huddled figures of the fishermen and their wives on the foreshore pointing out to the sea (the back of the stage).

'See,' one cried with his arm extended, 'there is lightning in yon sky.' (I was the lightning and that my cue for it): 'God help all the poor souls at sea tonight!' Then a woman cried, 'Look! Look! a boat upon the reef!' And as she said it I had to rush round and work the boat to make it go up and down properly. Then there was more lightning, and some one screamed out, 'Look! See! There's a woman in the boat!'

There wasn't really; it was me; but in the darkness it was all the same, and of course the heroine herself couldn't be there yet because she had to be downstairs getting dressed to be drowned. Then they all cried out, 'Poor soul! she's doomed,' and all the fishermen ran up and down making a noise.

Fishermen in those plays used to get fearfully excited; and what with the excitement and the darkness and the bright beams of the lighthouse falling on the wet oilskins, and the thundering of the sea upon the reef—ah! me, those were plays! That was acting! And to think that there isn't a single streak of lightning in any play on the boards this year!

And then the kind of climax that a play like this used to have! The scene shifted right at the moment of the excitement, and lo! we are in the tower, the top story of the lighthouse, interior scene. All is still and quiet within, with the bright light of the reflectors flooding the little room, and the roar of the storm heard like muffled thunder outside.

The lighthouse keeper trims his lamps. How firm and quiet and rugged he looks. The snows of sixty winters are on his head, but his eye is clear and his grip strong. Hear the howl of the wind as he opens the door and steps forth upon the iron balcony, eighty feet above the water, and peers out upon the storm.

'God pity all the poor souls at sea!' he says. (They all say that. If you get used to it, and get to like it, you want to hear it said, no matter how often they say it.) The waves rage beneath him. (I threw it at him, really, but the effect was wonderful.)

And then, as he comes in from the storm to the still room, the climax breaks. A man staggers into the room in oilskins, drenched, wet, breathless. (They all staggered in these plays, and in the new drama they walk, and the effect is feebleness itself.) He points to the sea. 'A boat! A boat upon the reef! With a woman in it.'

And the lighthouse keeper knows that it is his only daughter—the only one that he has—who is being cast to death upon the reef. Then comes the dilemma. They want him for the lifeboat; no one can take it through the surf but him. You know that because the other man says so himself.

But if he goes in the boat then the great light will go out. Untended it cannot live in the storm. And if it goes out—ah! If it goes out—ask of the angry waves and the resounding rocks of what tonight's long toll of death must be without the light!

I wish you could have seen it—you who only see the

drawing room plays of today—the scene when the lighthouse man draws himself up, calm and resolute, and says: 'My place is here. God's will be done.' And you know that as he says it and turns quietly to his lamps again, the boat is drifting, at that very moment, to the rocks.

'How did they save her?' My dear sir, if you can ask that question you little understand the drama as it was. Save her? No, of course they didn't save her. What we wanted in the Old Drama was reality and force, no matter how wild and tragic it might be. They did not save her. They found her the next day, in the concluding scene—all that was left of her when she was dashed upon the rocks. Her ribs were broken. Her bottom boards had been smashed in, the gunwale was gone—in short, she was a wreck.

The girl? Oh, yes, certainly they saved the girl. That kind of thing was always taken care of. You see just as the lighthouse man said 'God's will be done,' his eye fell on a long coil of rope, hanging there. Providential, wasn't it? But then we were not ashamed to use Providence in the Old Drama. So he made a noose in it and threw it over the balcony and hauled the girl up on it. I used to hook her on to it every night.

A rotten play? Oh, I am sure it must have been. But, somehow, those of us who were brought up on that sort of thing, still sigh for it.

Pause

I would advise a man to pause
Before he takes a wife;
Indeed, and I can see no cause
He should not pause for life.

Pierre Marivaux

Sigh No More, Ladies

Sigh no more, ladies, sigh no more,
Men were deceivers ever;
One foot on sea, and one on shore,
To one thing constant never.

Thomas Percy

Drunkards of Distinction

*Being A Brief Catalogue of
Eminent Topers, Lushes and Soaks*

The roll of notable British drunkards is a long one. It begins far back. No doubt the island climate is to blame.

This being but a brisk seasonable selection it is hardly necessary to apologise for omissions, even of some of your favourite topers, lushes and soaks.

Let us begin, then, with some of our alcoholic rulers. Certainly one of the earliest must be Bonosus, a late Roman governor who hanged himself in a fit of maudlin remorse after a particularly disgraceful defeat by the Picts. His troops made brutal, typically heavy Roman jokes on the lines of: 'There hangs a wineskin.'

Bonosus used to get drunk on the rough, heady Falernian red, which he imported straight from Tuscany. Meanwhile the grape vines and viticulture had been introduced into the island by St. Augustine's missionaries who needed wine handy for communion. Attached to the monasteries were vineyards which produced excellent British wines, thought to be not unlike still champagne and burgundies. But by the 9th century the import of wine was big enough to be worth taxing.

The coarse Saxon invaders preferred mead, beer, and crude

spirits which produced a savage hangover, known in Old English literature as 'ayenbite of inwit.' It proved too much for the native Britons. There is a story that Hengist got the British King, Vortigern, so stewed that he gave away the county of Kent.

The Danes also laid an early foundation to their universal reputation as big boozers. Hardicanute blew up at a wedding breakfast and fell to earth with a terrible convulsion. As for Canute, he was certainly not sober when he tried that megalomaniac experiment with the tide. 'Half seas over, I should say,' remarked one of his courtiers.

With the Norman invasion, wine again became the ruling class drink. The Conqueror was sober, but his son, William Rufus, besides alas, being given to importuning male persons in the New Forest, was a chronic alcoholic and hopelessly drunk when the arrow got him.

The three sons of Henry II were all drinkers. Geoffrey was a hopeless lush. Richard Cæur de Lion hit the bottle hard without letting it master him. John couldn't hold his and blew up.

British vineyards, meanwhile, were put out of big business by the fact that from 1152, for three centuries onwards, the Bordeaux claret-country belonged to the English crown. Prices make your mouth water. In the 12th century claret retailed in London at ld. Per gallon; in the 13th century at 2d.; in the 14th at 3½d., in the 16th at 8d.

◆

Among the Plantagenets, Edward II and Richard II tippled conscientiously, especially Edward II who qualifies for the lush class. Henry V drank hard. And for the Tudors, Henry VIII enjoyed periods, lasting sometimes for several days, of total intoxication.

James I was certainly a toper, if not a lush, though we

should not be too hard on him for he was but following the example of his nurse and his tutor. He was also, on occasion, led away by his brother-in-law Christian IV, King of Denmark.

Christian's visit to London in 1606 was the occasion of a tremendous booze-up at which, according to a contemporary letter:

> The two Monarchs embraced each other so lovingly that remarks were passed. The Nobles wallowed 'in beastly delights.' The ladies abandoned all sobriety and were seen to roll about in intoxication...King James, attempting to dance with the lady who was playing the part of the Queen of Sheba in a masque of Solomon's temple, passed out cold and was laid on a state bed. The ladies representing Peace, Hope, and Charity followed suit...

Cromwell's son, Dick, hardly counts as a ruler though he was midway between lush and soak. Charles I was a persistent bibber, though not a lush. Queen Anne was fond of brandy, in a quiet way, though not so fond of it as her obscure consort who belongs to the special category of Steady Silent Soaks.

It was not until the end of the 17th century that the impressed flush cork, together with that epoch-making invention the corkscrew, ushered in a period when really heavy drinking could be combined with connoisseurship.

The first two Hanoverians, though no blue-riband boys, were not particularly boozy nor was poor manic-depressive-George III. George IV was indubitably a toper, especially fond of brandy and sticky French liqueurs which he swigged at the oddest hours. He was seen more than once flat out in public. You could count him as a lush, or even a soak if you were feeling harsh. His brother William—Sailor Billy was a breezy open-air type of toper.

Queen Victoria's moderation was beyond reproach; her attitude toward drink was entirely rational. She told Gladstone to warn Canon Wilberforce, when preaching at Westminster, to lay off 'the very strong total abstinence language which he has carried to such an extreme hitherto. Total abstinence is an impossibility; and though it may be necessary in individual cases it will not do to insist on it as a general practice.'

◆

Of alcohol-addicted ecclesiastics you could mention Cardinal Wolsey, who was put in the stocks for drunkenness in his youth. And you must not forget Richard Corbett, Bishop of Oxford, in the 17th century, who got drunk with some ballad-singers one market day and sang with them at Abingdon Cross. He and his chaplain, Dr Lushington, used sometimes to lock themselves in the episcopal wine cellar for days at a time. Spare a moment, too, for the Elizabethan Dean Nonell of St. Paul's, thought by some to have been the accidental inventor of bottled beer.

Among 18th century divines there were some notable drunkards, among them the Rev. Parnell, who could not finish a sermon without stooping down in the pulpit every few sentences to fortify himself. There were still heavy drinking clerics of the sporting parson type in the 19th century, such as the Cornish vicar whom Benson visited soon after he took over the new bishopric of Truro. While he was trying, vainly, to get him to discuss church matters, the butler entered and asked what wine he should put out for communion? 'Damn it,' roared the vicar, 'let's give 'em hock for a change.'

The aristocracy has always been renowned for its single mindedness in this field. As you know, the all-time record for drunkenness among peers, or for that matter among poets another highly addicted group is held by the Earl of Rochester, most dissolute of all the Restoration Rakes, who was well away continuously for five on end.

◆

Among the drunkenest of Rochester's cronies were Sackville, later Earl of Dorset, and Sir Charles Sedley. Together with Sir Thomas Ogles, they were fined for indecently exposing themselves, after dinner, to the public from a balcony in Covent Garden. A play written by Sackville had to be taken off after the third act, as the cast had become incapable, the author's lines calling for almost continuous punch-drinking, and he having generously provided real punch for the actors.

Politicians and lawyers are supposed to need the full possession of their faculties, but there have been some notably bibulous figures among them. Brandy is generally their stand-by; you used to be able to smell it coming from the windows of the younger Pitt's coach as it rolled round Parliament Square after a late session. As for Fox, his liver was so hard that when they opened him up after death the surgeons rang guineas on it.

The record toper in the category is undoubtedly Sheridan, In the hardest drinking period of English history he outdrank them all. There was no limit to his capacity for wine. During his famous 24-hour speech in the House of Commons on the impeachment of Warren Hastings, he drank a gallon of brandy. He must somehow have communicated his intoxication to his audience for they declared that the speech was the most brilliant oration ever delivered at Westminster. It reads today as dully as a laundry list endlessly repeated.

An omnibib of equal capacity with Sheridan was the great

scholar Richard Porson, of whom it was said that he would sooner drink ink than nothing. He preferred port or brandy, but was known on occasion to down lamp-oil, embrocation, and the spirits of wine in which anatomical specimens had been preserved.

Literary men display a high proportion of topers, lushes and soaks. The problem generally is how precisely to classify them. The poets Occleve, Chaucer and Skelton (himself a wine merchant's son) were all topers, though not necessarily chronics. Shakespeare, in his youth, drank for the Stratford Boozers in an away match against the Sidbury Sippers and passed out under a tree. His death was brought on by a visit, when he was yet convalescent, from Ben Jonson and Drayton. They kept the delicate Swan of Avon out of bed swigging sack and canary and he folded.

Marvell wrote his poems on claret. The priggish Addison complained of ghastly hangovers. Steel was a chronic lush. Dr Johnson was a three bottle (port) man before he gave it up. He held his drink splendidly, unlike Boswell who passed out more than once on the pavement and was pulled in by the watch.

The fact that Lamb, the gentle Elia, was often stewed as an eel has been carefully kept from generations of schoolboys.

From *Lilliput*

Company

By Aimor A. Dickson

One night in late October
When I was far from sober,
Returning with my load with manly pride,
My feet began to stutter
So I lay down in the gutter,
And a pig came near and lay down by my side.
A lady passing by was heard then plain to say,
'You can tell a man who boozes,
By the company he chooses,'
At which the pig got up and slowly walked away.

Wimpole's Woe

By Louis Golding

Abert Wimpole was the sort of little man concerning whom women nudge each other in omnibuses and say, 'What a nice kind face he's got!' He was too kind to be a success as a business man, too industrious to be a success as a bricklayer, too tiny to make a good thing out of odd jobs in Covent Garden. So he became, because even editors could not resist his nice kind face, a literary critic.

He became the nicest and kindest literary critic in London. He found something of novelty in the most laboriously stereotyped novel, a certain lightness of touch in the most thunderous of sermons. Even about minor poetry he could not bring himself to be unkind. As he wrote his criticism he had a feeling that the author he was treating stood by his elbow with clasped hands and beseeching eyes. He could no more bring himself to say an unkind word about the book before him than he could have pushed its author into a vat of hot oil.

So he went on from season to season, finding somehow, somewhere, a little extenuation for the jejune, the lewd, the preposterous. A split infinitive might perhaps earn a gentle rebuke, but he would promptly apologise for his temerity by drawing attention to the author's delicacy or profundity. A nice kind critic.

And then one morning a volume appeared on Wimpole's table titled *Gangrene and Lilies*, the author being Mr Eustace Chasuble. I want to insist on this—Wimpole had not, as the saying is, got out of bed the wrong side that morning. His landlady had not scorched the bacon. He suffered occasionally from gumboils, but he was free at that time from that minor, but unpleasing affliction. Yet the fact remains that even as he unwrapped the book from the parcel, he felt that *Gangrene and Lilies* gave off an offensive odour. It stank. It was a volume of verses, an astonishing amalgam of the jejune, the lewd, the preposterous. No book had ever affected Wimpole in this desperate fashion before. It made him blink, his ears burned with shame, his gorge rose. And he sat down and wrote about it. All the ferocity he had suppressed for years blazed into one tempest of denunciation. (Is not the nicest and kindest little man in the world fundamentally a shrieking ape from the primordial jungles?) Whatever in the past he might have said about all the authors he had been nice and kind to, he now heaped upon Eustace Chasuble. And lots more. The sheets of paper flew from his pen like sparks from a knife-grinder's wheel. Wimpole grunted. Wimpole sweated. Then he sent his landlady's small daughter to the post with the completed jeremiad, and lay back on his chair and wept.

I assure you it was not the last time that Eustace Chasuble dissolved little Wimpole into a pool of tears. It was not the last time that Chasuble's large-eyed phantom came reproachfully into the room and stood beside Wimpose and wrung its hands and moaned. Poor little Wimpole! He could not have felt a more consummate blackguard if he had murdered his grandmother.

Waves of repentance surged over him and drowned him. Not a single word he had ever written could have so much as troubled a fly's wing. And now...And now...He beat his bosom.

He sometimes wondered whether his review had caused Eustace Chasuble to commit suicide. He paraded various methods of suicide in grisly pageantry before him. Chasuble hanging from a beam, his lips and tongue purple...Chasuble contorted in the unspeakable anguish of strychnine...Chasuble a dismembered corpse in the wake of the great North express. But always the original picture asserted itself in the end, the large-eyed phantom that came reproachfully into the room and stood beside him and wrung its hands and moaned.

He developed in his mind an extraordinary precise picture of Fustace Chasuble. He was about five feet four inches in height, his head was pear-shaped and rather too big for his body. The hair was long and jet black, the lips a vivid scarlet upon a sallow face. The finger-nails were long and (if the truth were told) a little dirty. He was knock-kneed. He had a fluting, high pitched voice. But his eyes, his reproachful, melancholy eyes... Wimpole lay back in his chair and sobbed.

Many years passed. Never again did Wimpole utter a word of criticism which was not in the last degree nice and kind. But he could not ever exorcise the phantom of Eustace Chasuble— the knock-kneed, long-haired, sad-eyed phantom of little Eustace Chasuble.

Behold him at this moment in the tiny market town of Bugmarsh, where he has a couple of hours to idle away before catching his connection for Town. He has been spending his annual fortnight's holiday in the heart of the country. But now the call of duty has gone forth and he must return to his labours. It is dusk. He is rather short-sighted. He is peering at the posters pasted up outside the parish hall of Bugmarsh. He learns that there is to be an auction sale of farm implements and effects next Tuesday, that to-morrow night an illustrious pianist from the Metropolis is actually going to honour Bugmarsh with his presence, that tonight—that tonight—O Heavens! No!

Wimpole's scalp froze. His hairs stood on end. As if to make it quite, quite certain that there could not be two Eustace Chasubles in the world, you were informed in chaste lettering under his name that he was the 'author of *Gangrene and Lilies*'. Mr Eustace Chasuble was to lecture that night, that very night, in the parish hall of Bugmarsh. His theme was to be—how blunt, how direct it was—'Pigs'. No more than that—'Pigs'. The lecture had started at seven o'clock. It was now half-past seven. Even if Eustace Chasuble continued for another hour there would be ample time to catch his train. Could he repudiate this opportunity, after so many years, to make amends? His heart filled with pity. Once more the phantom of little Chasuble stretched out its hands, stared mournfully and reproachfully upon him. Perhaps it was his own vitriolic review that had driven little Chasuble from the rivers of poetry (even though he had made them smell like sewers) and caused him to abandon lilies for mangel-wurzels, gazelles for pigs.

No, he must express his regrets for his intolerable unkindness. At last, at last, the chance he had not dared to hope for had been granted him. True that Chasuble had not thrown himself before a train or tossed off a flask of strychnine. But what if he bore with him to the grave a crushed, a broken heart?

'Pigs'...a curious theme...

Wimpole pushed his way through the door and across a vestibule. He heard a voice, assured and resonant. The chairman had obviously not finished his introductory remarks. Wimpole pushed open another door. It squeaked frightfully. A hundred large faces turned towards him, large as a harvest moon and red as an apple—ninety-eight in the hall, two upon the platform. A hundred pairs of eyes concentrated upon Wimpole. A wild instinct of flight seized him. All these healthy faces, these breeches and gaiters and leggings and side-whiskers...There was one empty chair in the middle of the room. The chairman pointed at it with a peremptory gesture. It must have been the lecturer he had interrupted, not the chairman. The chairman sat in the centre of the table before a bell and a flask. The lecturer held a bundle of notes in his hands and resumed his interrupted flow.

He roared, he bellowed, like the bull of Bashan. Not because he was angry with anything or anybody, but because that was his natural mode of utterance. He was a genial gentleman and hearty. He must have stood six foot and one or two inches in his stockinged feet. But he looked smaller because of the enormous bulk of his shoulders. He had huge red hands. His knees were like the nobbly ends of lopped branches on the trunk of an oak.

There was an especial species of pig, one gathered, that had won Mr Eustace Chasuble's affections. It was entitled the 'Large Black Pig'.

He recommended its virtues to his audience. His audience shook their heads in slow and weighty approbation, and tapped with their gnarled sticks on the ground. 'No breed,' proclaimed Mr Chasuble, 'could achieve such popularity without genuine merit, in the production both of pork and bacon: in the production of those cuts known as 'Medium', 'Fat', or 'Lean Sizeable'...'

Slowly a sweat of terror gathered upon Wimpole's brow. He tried to rise from his chair. The chair grated on the floor. He stumbled over somebody's stick. A hundred pairs of eyes concentrated upon him once more. The chairman touched the bell. Wimpole relapsed upon his chair. His heart tolled a muffled dirge within him. Mr Chasuble returned to the Large Black Pig.

'The great weight to which the Large Black Pig was bred formerly has now given way to greater quality, and at an early age it yields a long, deep-sided carcass of 160 lb. to 190 lb. dead weight, light in the shoulder, jowl, and offal...'

'They can't stop me,' thought Wimpole, 'slinking away when it's all over. God help me!'

But the lecture drew to an end and questions followed, and votes of thanks followed those, and the farmers ambled out of the hall. But little Wimpole still sat upon his chair like one hypnotised, his pale grey eyes staring from his head.

'Now's your chance to escape!' said Wimpole to himself. But his limbs would not obey him. A palsy, a terror had descended upon him. He was aware that Eustace Chasuble came striding like a tree over to him. Chasuble opened his mouth and spoke.

'If it's some more advice about the Large Black Pig you're wanting, sir...'

Then suddenly Wimpole found words, or words found Wimpole. He must now and for ever deliver himself from this phantom, even though the phantom had taken to itself so strange and terrible a shape.

'Your book of poems,' he cried, 'called *Gangrene and Lilies*. It was me. I wrote the review. My name's Wimpole! Sir, I assure you...'

'You!' exclaimed the other. 'So you're Wimpole!'

Wimpole saw his vast arm shoot through the air towards him like Jove's thunderbolt. He ducked. He found his tiny fingers crushed in a gigantic hand.

'I've been wanting to meet you for years, Mr Wimpole!' the vast voice boomed. 'The only critic who took any notice of my book. Thank you, Mr Wimpole, thank you! I can't say how grateful I am! Come round to the Pig and Whistle and let me try and tell you! No! Mr Wimpole, no! I'll take no refusals!' Mr Wimpole blinked.

My Failed Omelettes—and Other Disasters

In nearly fifty years of writing for a living, I have never succeeded in writing a best-seller. And now I know why. I can't cook.

Had I been able to do so, I could have turned out a few of those sumptuous looking cookery books that brighten up the bookstore windows before being snapped up by folk who can't cook either.

As it is, if I were forced to write a cook book, it would probably be called 'Fifty Different Ways of Boiling an Egg and Other Disasters'.

I used to think that boiling an egg would be a simple undertaking. But when I came to live at 7,000 ft in the Himalayan foothills, I found that just getting the water to boil was something of an achievement. I don't know if it's the altitude or the density of the water, but it just won't come to the boil in time for breakfast. As a result my eggs are only half-boiled. 'Never mind,' I tell everyone; 'half-boiled eggs are more nutritious than full-boiled eggs.'

'Why boil them at all?' asks my five-year old grandson, Gautam, who is my Mr Dick, always offering good advice. 'Raw eggs are probably healthier.'

'Just you wait and see,' I told him. 'I'll make you a cheese omelette you'll never forget.' And I did. It was a bit messy, as I was over-generous with the tomatoes, but I thought it tasted rather good. Gautam, however, pushed his plate away, saying, 'You forgot to put in the egg.'

'101 Failed Omelettes' might well be the title of my best-seller.

◆

I love watching other people cook—a habit that I acquired at a young age, when I would watch my Granny at work in the kitchen, turning out delicious curries, koftas and custards. I would try helping her, but she soon put a stop to my feeble contributions. On one occasion she asked me to add a cup of spices to a large curry dish she was preparing, and absent mindedly I added a cup of sugar. The result—a very sweet curry! Another invention of mine.

I was better at remembering Granny's kitchen proverbs. Here are some of them:

'There is skill in all things, even in making porridge.'

'Dry bread at home is better then curried prawns abroad.'

'Eating and drinking should not keep men from thinking.'

'Better a small fish than an empty dish.'

And her favourite maxim, with which she reprimanded me whenever I showed signs of gluttony: 'Don't let your tongue cut your throat.'

And as for making porridge, it's certainly no simple matter. I made one or two attempts, but it always came out lumpy.

'What's this?' asked Gautam suspiciously, when I offered him some.

'Porridge!' I said enthusiastically. 'It's eaten by those brave Scottish Highlanders who were always fighting the English!'

'And did they win?' he asked.

'Well-er—not usually. But they were outnumbered!'

He looked doubtfully at the porridge. 'Some other time,' he said.

So why not take the advice of Thoreau and try to simplify life? Simplify, simplify! Or simply sandwiches...

These shouldn't be too difficult, I decided. After all, they are basically bread and butter. But have you tried cutting bread into thin slices? Don't. It's highly dangerous. If you're a pianist, you could be putting your career at great risk.

You must get your bread ready sliced. Butter it generously. Now add your fillings. Cheese, tomato, lettuce, cucumber, whatever. Gosh, I was really going places! Slap another slice of buttered bread over this mouth-watering assemblage. Now cut in two. Result: Everything spills out at the sides and on to the table-cloth.

'Now look what you've gone and done,' says Gautam, in his best Oliver Hardy manner.

'Never mind,' I tell him. 'Practice makes perfect!'

And one of these days you're going to find 'Bond's Book of Better Sandwiches' up there on the best-seller lists.

Song for a Beetle in a Goldfish Bowl

A beetle fell into the goldfish bowl,
Hey-ho!
The beetle began to struggle and roll,
Ho-hum!
The window was open, the moon shone bright,
The crickets were singing with all their might,
But a blundering beetle had muddled his flight
And here he was now, in a watery plight,
Having given the goldfish a terrible fright,
Ho-hum, hey-ho!

The beetle swam left, the beetle swam right,
Hum-ho!
Along came myself—I said, 'Lord, what a sight!
That poor old beetle will drown tonight.
Ho-hum.
A beetle is just an insect, I hear,
But what if I fell in a vat full of beer?
I'd be brewed to light lager if no one came near—
(It happened I'm told, to a man in Tangier)—
Ho-hum, ho-hum.'

With my finger and thumb
The beetle I seized,
The goldfish looked pleased,
The window was open, the moon shone bright,
I thrust the beetle far out in the night,
And he bumbled away in a staggering flight,
Ho-hum, hey-ho,
Good night!

The Inn and the Dog

By Jerome K. Jerome

A thing that vexes much the high-class Anglo-Saxon soul is the earthly instinct prompting the German to fix a restaurant at the goal of every excursion. On mountain summit, in fairy glen, on lonely pass, by waterfall or winding stream, stands ever the busy Wirtschaft. How can one rhapsodize over a view when surrounded by beer-stained tables? How lose one's self in historical reverie amid the odour of roast veal and spinach?

One day, on elevating thoughts intent, we climbed through tangled woods.

'And at the top', said Harris, bitterly, as we paused to breathe a space and pull our belts a hole tighter, 'there will be a gaudy restaurant, where people will be guzzling beefsteaks and plum tarts and drinking white wine.'

'Do you think so?' said George.

'Sure to be,' answered Harris; 'you know their way. Not one grove will they consent to dedicate to solitude and contemplation; not one height will they leave to the lover of nature unpolluted by the gross and the material.'

'I calculate,' I remarked, 'that we shall be there a little before one o'clock, provided we don't dawdle.'

'The "mittagstisch" will be just ready,' groaned Harris, 'with possibly some of those little blue trout they catch about here. In Germany one never seems able to get away from food and drink. It is maddening!'

We pushed on, and in the beauty of the walk forgot our indignation. My estimate proved to be correct.

At a quarter to one, said Harris, who was leading:

'Here we are; I can see the summit.'

'Any sign of that restaurant?' said George.

'I don't notice it,' replied Harris; 'but it's there, you may be sure; confound it!'

Five minutes later we stood on the top. We looked north, south, east and west; then we looked at one another.

'Grand view, isn't it?' said Harris.

'Magnificent,' I agreed.

'Superb,' remarked George.

'They have had the good sense for once,' said Harris, 'to put that restaurant out of sight.'

'They do seem to have hidden it,' said George.

'One doesn't mind the thing so much when it is not forced under one's nose,' said Harris.

'Of course, in its place', I observed, 'a restaurant is right enough.'

'I should like to know where they *have* put it,' said George.

'Suppose we look for it?' said Harris, with inspiration.

It seemed a good idea. I felt curious myself. We agreed to explore in different directions, returning to the summit to report progress. In half an hour we stood together once again. There was no need for words. The face of one and all of us announced plainly that at last we had discovered a recess of German nature untarnished by the sordid suggestion of food or drink.

'I should never have believed it possible,' said Harris; 'would you?'

'I should say,' I replied, 'that this is the only square quarter of a mile in the entire Fatherland unprovided with one.'

'And we three strangers have struck it,' said George, 'without an effort.'

'True,' I observed. 'By pure good fortune we are now enabled to feast our finer senses undisturbed by appeal to our lower nature. Observe the light upon those distant peaks; is it not ravishing?'

'Talking of nature,' said George, 'which should you say was the nearest way down?'

'The road to the left,' I replied, after consulting the guide book, 'takes us to Sonnensteig—where, by the by, I observe the 'Goldener Adler' is well spoken of—in about two hours. The road to the right, though somewhat longer, commands more extensive prospects.'

One prospect, said Harris, 'is very much like another prospect; don't you think so?'

'Personally', George, 'I am going by the lefthand road.' And Harris and I went after him.

But we were not to get down so soon as we anticipated. Storms come quickly in these regions, and before we had walked for a quarter of an hour it became a question of seeking shelter or living for the rest of the day in soaked clothes. We decided on the former alternative, and selected a tree that, under ordinary circumstances, should have been ample protection. But a Black Forest thunderstorm is not an ordinary circumstance. We consoled ourselves at first by telling each other that at such a rate it could not last long. Next, we endeavoured to comfort ourselves with the reflection that if it did we should soon be too wet to fear getting wetter.

'As it turned out,' said Harris, 'I should have been almost glad if there had been a restaurant up here.'

'I see no advantage in being both wet and hungry,' said George. 'I should give it another five minutes, then I am going on.'

'These mountain solitudes', I remarked, 'are very attractive in fine weather. On a rainy day, especially if you happen to be past the age when—'

At this point there hailed us a voice, proceeding from a stout gentleman, who stood some fifty feet away from us under a big umbrella.

'Won't you come inside?' asked the stout gentleman

'Inside where?' I called back. I thought at first he was one of those fools that will try to be funny when there is nothing to be funny about.

'Inside the restaurant,' he answered.

We left our shelter and made for him. We wished for further information about this thing.

'I did call you from the window,' said the stout gentleman, as we drew near to him, 'but I suppose you did not hear me. This storm may last for another hour; you will get so wet.'

He was a kindly old gentleman; he seemed quite anxious about us.

I said: 'It is very kind of you to have come out. We are not lunatics. We have not been standing under that tree for the last half-hour knowing all the time there was a restaurant, hidden by the trees, within twenty yards of us. We had no idea we were anywhere near a restaurant.'

'I thought maybe you hadn't,' said the old gentleman; 'that is why I came.'

It appeared that all the people in the inn had been watching us from the windows, also wondering why we stood there looking miserable. If it had not been for this nice old gentleman the fools would have remained watching us, I suppose, for the rest of the afternoon. The landlord excused himself by saying he thought we looked like English. It is no figure of speech. On the Continent they do sincerely believe that every Englishman is mad. They are as convinced of it as is every English peasant that Frenchmen live on frogs. Even when one makes a direct personal effort to disabuse them of the impression one is not always successful.

It was a comfortable little restaurant, where they cooked well, while the Tischwein was really most passable. We stopped there for a couple of hours, and dried ourselves and fed ourselves, and talked about the view; and just before we left an incident occurred that shows how much more stirring in this world are the influences of evil compared with those of good.

A traveller entered. He seemed a careworn man. He carried a brick in his hand, tied to a piece of rope. He entered nervously and hurriedly, closed the door carefully behind him, saw to it that it was fastened, peered out of the window long and earnestly, and then, with a sigh of relief, laid his brick upon the bench beside him and called for food and drink.

There was something mysterious about the whole affair. One wondered what he was going to do with the brick, why he had closed the door so carefully, why he had looked so anxiously from the window; but his aspect was too wretched to invite conversation, and we forebore, therefore, to ask him questions. As he ate and drank he grew more cheerful, sighed less often. Later he stretched his legs, lit an evil-smelling cigar, and puffed in calm contentment.

Then it happened. It happened too suddenly for any detailed explanation of the thing to be possible. I recollect a Fräulein entering the room from the kitchen with a pan in her hand. I saw her cross to the outer door. The next moment the whole room was in an uproar. One was reminded of those pantomime transformation scenes where, from among floating clouds, slow music, waving flowers, and reclining fairies, one is suddenly transported into the midst of shouting policemen tumbling over yelling babies, swells fighting pantaloons, sausages and harlequins, buttered slides and clowns. As the Fraulein of the pan touched the door it flew open, as though all the spirits of sin had been pressed against it, waiting. Two pigs and a chicken rushed into the room; a cat that had been sleeping on a beer barrel spluttered into fiery life. The Fräulein threw her pan into the air and lay down on the floor. The gentleman with the brick sprang to his feet, upsetting the table before him with everything upon it.

One looked to see the cause of the disaster; one discovered it at once in the person of a mongrel terrier with pointed ears and a squirrel's tail. The landlord rushed out from another door, and attempted to kick him out of the room. Instead, he kicked one of the pigs, the fatter of the two. It was a vigorous, well planted kick, and the pig got the whole of it, none of it was wasted. One felt sorry for the poor animal; but no amount of sorrow anyone else might feel for him could compare with the sorrow he felt for himself. He stopped running about; he sat down in the middle of the room, and appealed to the solar system generally to observe the unjust thing that had come upon him. They must have heard this complaint in the valleys round about, and have wondered what upheaval of nature was taking place among the hills.

As for the hen it scuttled, screaming, every way at once. It was a marvelous bird; it seemed to be able to run up a straight wall quite easily; and it and the cat between them fetched down most everything that was not already on the floor. In less than forty seconds there were nine people in that room, all trying to kick one dog. Possibly, now and again, one or another may have succeeded, for occasionally the dog would stop barking in order to howl. But it did not discourage him. Everything has to be paid for, he evidently argued, even a pig and chicken hunt; and, on the whole, the game was worth it.

Besides, he had the satisfaction of observing that, for every kick he received, most other living things in the room got two. As for the unfortunate pig—the stationary one, the one that still sat lamenting in the centre of the room—he must have averaged a steady four. Trying to kick this dog was like playing football with a ball that was never there—not when you went to kick it, but after you had started to kick it, and had gone too far to stop yourself, so that the kick had to go on in any case, your only hope being that your foot would find something or another solid to stop it, and so save you from sitting down on the floor noisily and completely. When anybody did kick the dog it was by pure accident, when they were not expecting to kick him; and, generally speaking, this took them so unawares that, after kicking him, they fell over him. And everybody, every half-minute, would be certain to fall over the pig—the sitting pig, the one incapable of getting out of anybody's way.

How long the scrimmage might have lasted it is impossible to say. It was ended by the judgment of George. For a while he had been seeking to catch, not the dog but the remaining pig, the one still capable of activity. Cornering it at last, he persuaded it to cease running round and round the room, and instead to take a spin outside. It shot through the door with one long wail.

We always desire the thing we have not. One pig, a chicken, nine people, and a cat, there was nothing in that dog's opinion compared with the quarry that was disappearing. Unwisely, he darted after it, and George closed the door on him and shot the bolt.

Then the landlord stood up and surveyed all the things that were lying on the floor.

'That's a playful dog of yours,' said he to the man who had come in with the brick.

'He's not my dog,' replied the man sullenly. 'Whose dog is it then?' said the landlord. 'I don't know whose dog it is,' answered the man.

'That won't do for me, you know,' said the landlord, picking up a picture of the German Emperor, and wiping beer from it with his sleeve.

'I know it won't,' replied the man. 'I never expected it would. I'm tired of telling people it isn't my dog. None of them believe me.'

'What do you want to go about with him for, if he's not your dog!' said the landlord. 'What's the attraction about him?'

'I don't go about with him,' replied the man; 'he goes about with me. He picked me up this morning at ten o'clock, and he won't leave me. I thought I had got rid of him when I came in here. I left him busy killing a duck more than a quarter of an hour away. I'll have to pay for that, I expect, on my way back.'

'Have you tried throwing stones at him?' asked Harris.

'Have I tried throwing stones at him!' replied the man contemptuously. 'I've been throwing stones at him till my arm aches with throwing stones; and he thinks it's a game, and brings them back to me. 'I've been carrying this beastly brick about with me for over an hour, in the hope of being able to drown him, but he never comes near enough for me to get hold of him. He just sits six inches out of reach with his mouth open and looks at me.'

'It's the funniest story I've heard for a long while,' said the landlord.

'Glad it amuses somebody,' said the man.

We left him helping the landlord to pick up the broken things and went our way. A dozen yards outside the doorway the faithful animal was waiting for his friend. He looked tired but contented.

From *Three Men On The Bummel*

The Ghost Ship

By Richard Middleton

Fairfield is a little village lying near the Portsmouth Road about half-way between London and the sea. Strangers who find it by accident now and then, call it a pretty, old-fashioned place; we, who live in it and call it home, don't find anything very pretty about it, but we should be sorry to live anywhere else. Our minds have taken the shape of the inn and the church and the green, I suppose. At all events we never feel comfortable out of Fairfield.

Of course the Cockneys, with their vasty houses and their noise-ridden streets, can call us rustics if they choose, but for all that Fairfield is a better place to live in than London. Doctor says that when he goes to London his mind is bruised with the weight of the houses, and he was a Cockney born. He had to live there himself when he was a little chap, but he knows better now. You gentlemen may laugh—perhaps some of you come from London way—but it seems to me that a witness like that is worth a gallon of arguments.

Dull? Well, you might find it dull, but I assure you that I've listened to all the London yarns you have spun tonight, and they're absolutely nothing to the things that happen at Fairfield. It's because of our way of thinking and minding our own business. If one of your Londoners were set down on the green of a Saturday night when the ghosts of the lads who died in the war keep tryst with the lasses who lie in the churchyard, he couldn't help being curious and interfering, and then the ghosts would go somewhere where it was quieter. But we just let them come and go and don't make any fuss, and in consequence Fairfield is the ghostiest place in all England. Why I've seen a headless man sitting on the edge of the well in broad daylight, and the children playing about his feet as if he were their father. Take my word for it, spirits know when they are well off as much as human beings.

Still, I must admit that the thing I'm going to tell you about was queer even for our part of the world, where three packs of ghost-hounds hunt regularly during the season, and blacksmith's great-grandfather is busy all night shoeing the dead gentlemen's horses. Now that's a thing that wouldn't happen in London, because of their interfering ways, but blacksmith he lies up aloft and sleeps as quiet as a lamb. Once when he had a bad head he shouted down to them not to make so much noise, and in the morning he found an old guinea left on the anvil as an apology. He wears it on his watch-chain now. But I must get on with my story; if I start telling you about the queer happenings at Fairfield I'll never stop.

It all came of the great storm in the spring of '97, the year that we had two great storms. This was the first one, and I remember it very well, because I found in the morning that it had lifted the thatch of my pigsty into the widow's garden as clean as a boy's kite. When I looked over the hedge, widow—Tom Lamport's widow that was—was prodding for her nasturtiums with a daisy-grubber. After I had watched her for a little I went down to the 'Fox and Grapes' to tell landlord what she had said to me. Landlord he laughed, being a married man and at ease with the sex. 'Come to that,' he said, 'the tempest has blowed something into my field. A kind of a ship I think it would be.'

I was surprised at that until he explained that it was only a ghost-ship and would do no hurt to the turnips. We argued that it had been blown up from the sea at Portsmouth, and then we talked of something else. There were two slates down at the parsonage and a big tree in Lumley's meadow. It was a rare storm.

I reckon the wind had blown our ghosts all over England. They were coming back for days afterwards with foundered horses and as footsore as possible, and they were so glad to get back to Fairfield that some of them walked up the street crying like little children. Squire said that his great-grandfather's great grandfather hadn't looked so dead-beat since the battle of Naseby, and he's an educated man.

What with one thing and another, I should think it was a week before we got straight again, and then one afternoon I met the landlord on the green and he had a worried face. 'I wish you'd come and have a look at that ship in my field,' he said to me;' it seems to me it's leaning real hard on the turnips. I can't bear thinking what the missus will say when she sees it.'

I walked down the lane with him, and sure enough there was a ship in the middle of his field, but such a ship as no man had seen on the water for three hundred years, let alone in the middle of a turnip-field. It was all painted black and covered with carvings, and there was a great bay window in the stern for all the world like the Squire's drawing-room. There was a crowd of little black cannon on deck and looking out of her port-holes, and she was anchored at each end to the hard ground.

I have seen the wonders of the world on picture-postcards, but I have never seen anything to equal that.

'She seems very solid for a ghost-ship,' I said, seeing the landlord was bothered.

'I should say it's a betwixt and between,' he answered, puzzling it over, 'but it's going to spoil a matter of fifty turnips, and missus she'll want it moved. We went up to her and touched the side, and it was as hard as a real ship. Now there's folks in England would call that very curious,' he said.

Now I don't know much about ships, but I should think that that ghost-ship weighed a solid two hundred tons, and it seemed to me that she had come to stay, so that I felt sorry for landlord, who was a married man. 'All the horses in Fairfield won't move her out of my turnips,' he said, frowning at her.

Just then we heard a noise on her deck, and we looked up and saw that a man had come out of her front cabin and was looking down at us very peaceably. He was dressed in a black uniform set out with rusty gold lace, and he had a great cutlass by his side in a brass sheath. 'I'm Captain Bartholomew Roberts,' he said, in a gentleman's voice, put in for recruits. 'I seem to have brought her rather far up the harbour.'

'Harbour!' cried landlord; 'why, you're fifty miles from the sea.'

Captain Robert didn't turn a hair. 'So much as that, is it?' he said coolly. 'Well, it's of no consequence.'

Landlord was a bit upset at this. 'I don't want to be unneighbourly,' he said, 'but I wish you hadn't brought your ship into my field. You see, my wife sets great store on these turnips.'

The Captain took a pinch of snuff out of a fine gold box that he pulled out of his pocket, and dusted his fingers with a silk handkerchief, in a very genteel fashion. 'I'm only here for a few months,' he said; 'but if a testimony of my esteem would pacify your good lady I should be content.' And with the words he loosed a great gold brooch from the neck of his coat and tossed it down to landlord.

Landlord blushed as red as a strawberry. 'I'm not denying she's fond of jewellery,' he said, 'but it's too much for half a sackful of turnips.' And indeed it was a handsome brooch.

The Captain laughed. 'Tut, man,' he said, 'it's a forced sale, and you deserve a good price. Say no more about it;' and nodding good-day to us, he turned on his heel and went into the cabin. Landlord walked back up the lane like a man with a weight off his mind. 'That tempest has blowed me a bit of luck,' he said; 'the missus will be main pleased with that brooch. It's better than the blacksmith's guinea any day.'

Ninety-seven was Jubilee year, the year of the second Jubilee, you remember, and we had great doings at Fairfield, so that we hadn't much time to bother about the ghost-ship, though anyhow it isn't our way to meddle in things that don't concern us. Landlord, he saw his tenant once or twice when he was hoeing his turnips and passed the time of day, and landlord's wife wore her new brooch to church every Sunday. But we didn't mix much with the ghosts at any time, all except an idiot lad there was in the village, and he didn't know the difference between a man and a ghost, poor innocent! On Jubilee Day, however, somebody told Captain Roberts why the church bells were ringing, and he hoisted a flag and fired off his guns like a loyal Englishman. 'Tis true the guns were shotted, and one of the round shot knocked a hole in Farmer Johnstone's barn, but nobody thought much of that in such a season of rejoicing.

It wasn't till our celebrations were over that we noticed that anything was wrong in Fairfield. 'Twas shoemaker who told me first about it one morning at the 'Fox and Grapes.' 'You know my great great-uncle' he said to me.

'You mean Joshua, the quiet lad,' I answered, knowing him well.

'Quiet!' said shoemaker indignantly. Quiet you call him, coming home at three o'clock every morning as drunk as a magistrate and waking up the whole house with his noise.

'Why, it can't be Joshua! I said, for I knew him for one of the most respectable young ghosts in the village.

Joshua it is,' said shoemaker; 'and one of these nights he'll find himself out in the street if he isn't careful.'

This kind of talk shocked me, I can tell you, for I don't like to hear a man abusing his own family, and I could hardly believe that a steady youngster like Joshua had taken to drink. But just then in came butcher Aylwin in such a temper that he could hardly drink his beer. 'The young puppy! The young puppy!' he kept on saying; and it was some time before shoemaker and I found out that he was talking about his ancestor that fell at Senlac.

'Drink?' said shoemaker hopefully, for we all like company in our misfortunes, and butcher nodded grimly.

'The young noodle,' he said, emptying his tankard.

Well, after that I kept my ears open, and it was the same story all over the village. There was hardly a young man among all the ghosts of Fairfield who didn't roll home in the small hours of the morning the worse for liquor. I used to wake up in the night and hear them stumble past my house, singing outrageous songs. The worst of it was that we couldn't keep the scandal to ourselves, and the folk at Greenhill began to talk of 'sodden Fairfield and taught their children to sing a song about us:

> Sodden Fairfield, sodden Fairfield, has no use for bread and-butter,
> Rum for breakfast, rum for dinner, rum for tea, and rum for supper!

We are easy-going in our village, but we didn't like that.

Of course we soon found out where the young fellows went to get the drink, and landlord was terribly cut up that his tenant should have turned out so badly, but his wife wouldn't hear of parting with the brooch, so that he couldn't give the Captain notice to quit. But as time went on, things grew from bad to worse, and at all hours of the day you would see those young reprobates sleeping it off on the village green. Nearly every afternoon a ghost-waggon used to jolt down to the ship with a lading of rum, and though the older ghosts seemed inclined to give the Captain's hospitality the go-by, the youngsters were neither to hold nor to bind.

So one afternoon when I was taking my nap I heard a knock at the door, and there was parson looking very serious, like a man with a job before him that he didn't altogether relish. 'I'm going down to talk to the Captain about all this drunkenness in the village, and I want you to come with me,' he said straight out.

I can't say that I fancied the visit much myself, and I tried to hint to parson that as, after all, they were only a lot of ghosts, it didn't very much matter.

'Dead or alive, I'm responsible for their good conduct,' he said, 'and I'm going to do my duty and put a stop to this continued disorder. And you are coming with me, John

Simmons.' So I went, parson being a persuasive kind of man.

We went down to the ship, and as we approached her I could see the Captain tasting the air on deck. When he saw parson he took off his hat very politely, and I can tell you that I was relieved to find that he had a proper respect for the cloth. Parson acknowledged his salute and spoke out stoutly enough. 'Sir, I should be glad to have a word with you.'

'Come on board, sir, come on board,' said the Captain, and I could tell by his voice that he knew why we were there. Parson and I climbed up an uneasy kind of ladder, and the Captain took us into the great cabin at the back of the ship, where the bay window was. It was the most wonderful place you ever saw in your life, all full of gold and silver plate, swords with jewelled scabbards, carved oak chairs, and great chests that looked as though they were bursting with guineas. Even parson was surprised, and he did not shake his head very hard when the Captain took down some silver cups and poured us out a drink of rum. I tasted mine, and I don't mind saying that it changed my view of things entirely. There was nothing betwixt and between about that rum, and I felt that it was ridiculous to blame the lads for drinking too much of stuff like that. It seemed to fill my veins with honey and fire.

Parson put the case squarely to the Captain, but I didn't listen much to what he said; I was busy sipping my drink and looking through the window at the fishes swimming to and fro over landlord's turnips. Just then it seemed the most natural thing in the world that they should be there, though afterwards, of course, I could see that that proved it was a ghost-ship.

But even then I thought it was queer when I saw a drowned sailor float by in the thin air with his hair and beard all full of bubbles. It was the first time I had seen anything quite like that at Fairfield.

All the time I was regarding the wonders of the deep, parson was telling Captain Roberts how there was no peace or rest in the village owing to the curse of drunkenness, and what a bad example the youngsters were setting to the older ghosts. The Captain listened very attentively, and only put in a word now and then about boys being boys and young men sowing their wild oats. But when parson had finished his speech he filled up our silver cups and said to parson, with a flourish. 'I should be sorry to cause trouble anywhere where I have been made welcome, and you will be glad to hear that I put to sea tomorrow night. And now you must drink me a prosperous voyage.' So we all stood up and drank the toast with honour, and that noble rum was like hot oil in my veins.

After that Captain showed us some of the curiosities he had brought back from foreign parts, and we were greatly amazed, though afterwards I couldn't clearly remember what they were. And when I found myself walking across the turnips with parson, and I was telling him of the glories of the deep that I had seen through the window of the ship. He turned on me severely. 'If I were you, John Simmons, he said, I should go straight home to bed.' He has a way of putting things that wouldn't occur to an ordinary man, has parson, and I did as he told me.

Well, next day it came on to blow, and it blew harder and harder, till about eight o'clock at night I heard a noise and looked out into the garden. I dare say you won't believe me, it seems a bit tall even to me, but the wind had lifted the thatch of my pigsty into the widow's garden a second time. I thought I wouldn't wait to hear what window had to say about it, so I went across the green to the 'Fox and Grapes', and the wind was so strong that I danced along on tip-toe like a girl at the fair. When I got to the inn landlord had to help me shut the door; it seemed as though a dozen goats were pushing against it to come in out of the storm.

'It's a powerful tempest,' he said, drawing the beer. 'I hear there's a chimney down at Dickory End.'

'It's a funny thing how these sailors know about the weather, I answered. 'When Captain said he was going tonight, I was thinking it would take a capful of wind to carry the ship back to sea, but now here's more than a capful.'

'Ah, yes,' said landlord, 'it's tonight he goes, true enough, and, mind you, though he treated me handsome over the rent, I'm not sure it's a loss to the village. I don't hold with gentrice who fetch their drink from London instead of helping local traders to get their living.'

'But you haven't got any rum like his,' I said to draw him out.

His neck grew red above his collar, and I was afraid I'd gone too far; but after a while he got his breath with a grunt.

'John Simmons,' he said, 'if you've come down here this windy night to talk a lot of fool's talk, you've wasted a journey.'

Well, of course, then I had to smooth him down with praising his rum and Heaven forgive me for swearing it was better than Captain's. For the like of that rum no living lips have tasted save mine and parson's. But somehow or other I brought landlord round, and presently we must have a glass of his best to prove its quality.

'Beat that if you can!' he carried, and we both raised our glasses to our mouths, only to stop half-way and look at each other in amaze. For the wind that had been howling outside like an outrageous dog had all of a sudden turned as melodious as the carol-boys of a Christmas Eve.

'Surely that's not my Martha,' whispered landlord; Martha being his great-aunt that lived in the loft overhead.

We went to the door, and the wind burst it open so that the handle was driven clean into the plaster of the wall. But we didn't think about that at the time; for over our heads, sailing very comfortably through the windy stars, was the ship that had passed the summer in landlord's field. Her port-holes and her bay-window were blazing with lights, and there was a noise of singing and fiddling on her decks. 'He's gone,' shouted landlord above the storm, 'and he's taken half the village with him!' I could only nod in answer, not having lungs like bellows of leather.

In the morning we were able to measure the strength of the storm, and over and above my pigsty there was damage enough wrought in the village to keep us busy. True it is that the children had to break down no branches for the firing that autumn, since the wind had strewn the woods with more than they could carry away. Many of our ghosts were scattered abroad, but this time very few came back, all the young men having sailed with Captain; and not only ghosts, for a poor half-witted lad was missing, and we reckoned that he had stowed himself away or perhaps shipped as cabin-boy, not knowing any better.

What with the lamentations of the ghost-girls and the grumblings of families who had lost an ancestor, the village was upset for a while, and the funny thing was that it was the folk who had complained most of the carryings—on of the youngsters, who made most noise now that they were gone. I hadn't any sympathy with shoemaker or butcher, who ran about saying how much they missed their lads, but it made me grieve to hear the poor bereaved girls calling their lovers by name on the village green at nightfall. It didn't seem fair to me that they should have lost their men a second time, after giving up life in order to join them, as like as not. Still, not even a spirit can be sorry for ever, and after a few months we made up our mind that the folk who had sailed in the ship were never coming back, and we didn't talk about it any more.

And then one day, I dare say it would be a couple of years after, when the whole business was quite forgotten, who should come trapesing along the road from Portsmouth but the daft lad who had gone away with the ship, without waiting till he was dead to become a ghost. You never saw such a boy as that in all your life. He had a great rusty cutlass hanging to a string at his waist, and he was tattooed all over in fine colours, so that even his face looked like a girl's sampler. He had a handkerchief in his hand full of foreign shells and old-fashioned pieces of small money, very curious, and he walked up to the well outside his mother's house and drew himself a drink as if he had been nowhere in particular.

The worst of it was that he had come back as soft-headed as he went, and try as we might we couldn't get anything reasonable out of him. He talked a lot of gibberish about keel hauling and walking the plank and crimson murders—things which a decent sailor should know nothing about, so that it seemed to me that for all his manners Captain had been more of a pirate than a gentleman mariner. But to draw sense out of that boy was as hard as picking cherries off a crab-tree. One silly tale he had that he kept on drifting back to, and to hear him you would have thought that it was the only thing that happened to him in his life. 'We was at anchor,' he would say, 'off an island called the Basket of Flowers, and the sailors had caught a lot of parrots and we were teaching them to swear. Up and down the decks, up and down the decks, and the language they used was dreadful. Then we looked up and saw the masts of the Spanish ship outside the harbour. Outside the harbour they were, so we threw the parrots into the sea and sailed out to fight. And all the parrots were drowned in the sea and the language they used was dreadful.' That's the sort of boy he was, nothing but silly talk of parrots when we asked him about the fighting. And we never had a chance of teaching him better, for two days after he ran away again, and hasn't been seen since.

That's my story, and I assure you that things like that are happening at Fairfield all the time. The ship has never come back, but somehow as people grow older they seem to think that one of these windy nights she'll come sailing in over the hedges with all the lost ghosts on board. Well, when she comes, she'll be welcome. There's one ghost-lass that has never grown tired of waiting for her lad to return. Every night you'll see her out on the green, straining her poor eyes with looking for the mast lights among the stars. A faithful lass you'd call her, and I'm thinking you'd be right.

Landlord's field wasn't a penny the worse for the visit, but they do say that since then the turnips that have been grown in it have tasted of rum.

About John

Who Lost a Fortune by Throwing Stones

By Hilaire Belloc

John Vavassour De Quentin Jones
Was very fond
Of throwing stones

At Horses, People,
Passing trains,
But specially at
Window-panes.

Like many of the
Upper Class
He liked the
Sound of
Broken
Glass[1]

It bucked him up and made him gay:
It was his favourite form of play.

---

[1] A line I stole with subtle daring
From Wing-Commander Maurice Baring.

But the Amusement cost him dear,
My children, as you now shall hear.

JOHN VAVASSOUR DE QUENTIN had
An uncle, who adored the lad:
And often chuckled, 'Wait until
You see what's left you in my will!'

Nor were the words without import,
Because this uncle did a sort
Of something in the City, which
Had made him fabulously rich.
(Although his brother, John's papa,
Was poor, as many fathers are.)

He had a lot of stocks and shares
And half a street in Buenos Aires,[2]
A bank in Rio, and a line
Of Steamers to the Argentine.
And options more than I can tell,
And bits of Canada as well;
He even had a mortgage on
The House inhabited by John.
His will, the cause of all the fuss,
Was carefully indited thus:

This is the last and solemn Will
Of Uncle William—known as Bill.

I do bequeath, devise and give
By Executive Mandative

---

[2]But this pronunciation varies. Some people call it Bu-enos Aires.

The whole amount of what I've got
(It comes to a tremendous lot!)
In seizin to devote upon
My well-beloved nephew John.

(And here the witnesses will sign
Their names upon the dotted line.)'

Such was the Legal Instrument
Expressing Uncle Bill's intent.

As time went on declining Health
Transmogrified this Man of Wealth;
And it was excellently clear
That Uncle Bill's demise was near.

At last his sole idea of fun
Was sitting snoozling in the sun.

So once, when he would take the air,
They wheeled him in his Patent Chair
(By 'They', I mean his Nurse, who came
From Dorchester upon the Thame:
Miss Charming was the Nurse's name),
To where beside a little wood
A long abandoned green-house stood,

And there he sank into a doze
Of senile and inept repose.
But not for long his drowsy ease!
A stone came whizzing through the trees,
And caught him smartly in the eye.
He woke with an appalling cry,

And shrieked in agonizing tones:
Oh! Lord! Whoever's throwing stones!

Miss Charming, who was standing near,
Said: 'That was Master John, I fear!

Go, get my Ink-pot and my Quill,
My Blotter and my Famous Will.'
Miss Charming flew as though on wings
To fetch these necessary things,
And Uncle William ran his pen
Through 'well-beloved John,' and then
Proceeded, in the place of same,
To substitute Miss Charming's name:
Who now resides in Portman Square
And is accepted everywhere.

Henry King

By Hilaire Belloc

The chief defect of Henry King
Was chewing little bits of string.
At last he swallowed some which tied
Itself in ugly Knots inside.
Physicians of the Utmost Fame
Were called at once; but when they came
They answered, as they took their Fees,
'There is no cure for this Disease.
Henry will very soon be dead.'
His Parents stood about his Bed
Lamenting his Untimely Death,
When Henry, with his Latest Breath,
Cried—
'Oh, my Friends, be warned by me,
That Breakfast, Dinner, Lunch and Tea
Are all the Human Frame requires...'
With that the Wretched Child expires.

Matilda

By Hilaire Belloc

Matilda told such Dreadful Lies,
It made one Gasp and Stretch one's Eyes;
Her Aunt, who, from her Earliest Youth,
Had kept a Strict Regard for Truth,
Attempted to Believe Matilda:
The effort very nearly killed her,
And would have done so, had not She
Discovered this Infirmity.
For once, towards the Close of Day,
Matilda, growing tired of play,
And finding she was left alone,
Went tiptoe to the Telephone
And summoned the Immediate Aid
Of London's Noble Fire-Brigade.
Within an hour the Gallant Band
Were pouring in on every hand,
From Putney, Hackney Downs and Bow,
With Courage high and Hearts a-glow
They galloped, roaring through the Town,

'Matilda's House is Burning Down!'
Inspired by British Cheers and Loud
Proceeding from the Frenzied Crowd,
They ran their ladders through a score
Of windows on the Ball Room Floor;
And took Peculiar Pains to Souse
The Pictures up and down the House,
Until Matilda's Aunt succeeded
In showing them they were not needed
And even then she had to pay
To get the Men to go away!

It happened that a few weeks later
Her Aunt was off to the Theatre
To see that Interesting Play
'The Second Mrs Tanqueray.'
She had refused to take her Niece
To hear this Entertaining Piece:
A Deprivation Just and Wise
To Punish her for Telling Lies.
That Night a Fire did break out
You should have heard Matilda Shout!
You should have heard her Scream and Bawl,
And throw the window up and call
To People passing in the Street—
(The rapidly increasing Heat
Encouraging her to obtain
Their confidence)—but all in vain!
For every time she shouted 'Fire!'
They only answered 'Little Liar!'
And therefore when her Aunt returned,
Matilda, and the House, were Burned.

The Dinner-Party

By E.V. Lucas

[The dinner-party was at Mr Wynne's, the father of Naomi whom Kent Falconer, the narrator of *Over Bemerton's*, marries. Mr Dabney was a Radical editor. Lionel is a county cricketer.]

When the evening arrived, it looked as though Grandmamma and Mr Dabney were going to hit it off perfectly, and I began to feel quite happy about my introduction of this firebrand into the household.

'I hear that you are a writer,' Grandmamma began, very graciously. 'I always like literary company. Years ago I met both Mr Dickens and Mr Thackeray.'

I saw the lid of Lionel's left eye droop as he glanced at Naomi. Mrs Wynne, I gathered, was employing a favourite opening.

Mr Dabney expressed interest.

'There are no books like theirs now,' Grandmamma continued. 'I don't know what kind of books you write, but there are no books like those of Mr Dickens and Mr Thackeray.'

Mr Dabney began to say something.

'Personally,' Grandmamma hurried on, 'I prefer those of

Mr Dickens, but that perhaps is because me dear fawther used to read them to us aloud. He was a beautiful reader. There is no reading aloud today, Mr Dabney; and, I fear, very little home life.'

Here Grandmamma made a false move and let her companion in, for he could never resist a comparison of the present and the past, to the detriment of the present.

'No,' he said, 'you are quite right.' And such was the tension that Grandmamma's remarks had caused that the whole room was silent for him. 'We are losing our hold, on all that is most precious. Take London at this moment—look at the scores and scores of attractions to induce people to leave home in the evenings and break up the family circle—restaurants, concert room, entertainments, theatres. Look at the music-halls. Do you know how many music-halls there are in London and Greater London at this moment?

'No,' said Grandmamma sternly, 'I have no notion. I have never entered one.'

Lionel shot a glance at me which distinctly said, in his own deplorable idiom, 'What price Alf Pinto?'

Mr Dabney, I regret to say, intercepted the tail of it, and suddenly realised that he was straying from the wiser path of the passive listener. So he remarked, 'Of course not,' and brought the conversation back to Boz.

'Mr Dickens,' said Grandmamma, 'did me the honour to converse with me in Manchester in the 'sixties. I was there with me dear husband on business, and we stayed in the same hotel as Mr Dickens, and breakfasted at the same table. The toast was not good, and Mr Dickens, I remember, compared it in his inimitable way to sawdust. It was a perfect simile. He was very droll. What particularly struck me about him was his eye—so bright and restless—and his quick ways. He seemed all nerves. In the course of our conversation I told him I had met Mr Thackeray, but he was not interested. I remember another thing he said. In paying his bill he gave the waiter a very generous tip, which was the slang word with which me dear husband always used to describe a douceur. 'There,' Mr Dickens said, as he gave it to the waiter, 'that's—' How very stupid! I have forgotten what he said, but it was full of wit. 'There,' he said... Dear me!'

'Never mind, Grandmamma,' said Naomi, 'you will think of it presently.'

'But it was so droll and clever,' said the old lady. 'Surely, Alderley dear, I have told you of it?'

'Oh, yes, Mother, many times,' said Alderley; 'but I can't for the life of me think of it at the moment. Strange, isn't it,' he remarked to us all at large, 'how often the loss of memory in one person seems to infect others—one forgets and all forget. We had a case in Chambers the other day.'

Their father's stories having no particular sting in them, his children abandoned him to their mother, who listens devotedly and we again fell into couples.

But it was useless to attempt disregard of old Mrs Wynne. There was a feeling in the air that trouble lay ahead, and we all reserved one ear for her.

'And Mr Thackeray?' Mr Dabney asked, with an appearance of the deepest interest..

'Mr Thackeray,' said Grandmamma, 'I had met in London some years before. It was at a conversazione at the Royal Society's. Mr Wynne and I were leaving at the same time as the great man—and however you may consider his writings he was great physically and there was a little confusion about the cab. Mr Thackeray thought it was his, and we thought it was ours. Me dear husband, who was the soul of courtesy, pressed him to take it; but Mr Thackeray gave way, with the most charming bow, to me. It was raining. A very tall man with a broad and kindly face—although capable of showing satire—and gold spectacles. He gave me a charming bow, and said, 'There will be another one for me directly.' I hope there was, for it was raining. Those were, however, his exact words: 'There will be another one for me directly.'

Mr Dabney expressed himself in suitable terms, and cast a swift glance, at his hostess on his other side, as if seeking for relief. She was talking, as it happened, about a novel of the day, in which little but the marital relation is discussed, and Mr Dabney, on being drawn into the discussion, remarked sententiously, 'The trouble with marriage is that while every woman is at heart a mother, every man is at heart a bachelor.'

'What was that?' said Grandmamma, who is not really deaf, but when in a tight place likes to gain time by this harmless imposition. 'What did Mr Dabney say?' she repeated, appealing to Naomi.

Poor Mr Dabney turned scarlet. To a mind of almost mischievous fearlessness is allied a shrinking sensitiveness and distaste for prominence of any kind, especially among people whom he does not know well.

'Oh, it was nothing, nothing,' he said. 'Merely a chance remark.'

'I don't agree with you,' replied Grandmamma severely, thus giving away her little ruse. 'There is no trouble with marriage. It is very distressing to find this new attitude with regard to that state. When I was a girl we neither talked about incompatibility and temperament and all the rest of it, nor thought about them. We married. I have had to give up my library subscription entirely because they send me nothing nowadays but nauseous novels about husbands and wives who cannot get on together. I hope,' she added, turning swiftly to Mr Dabney, 'that those are not the kind of books that you write.'

'Oh, no,' said Mr Dabney; 'I don't write books at all.'

'Not write books at all?' said Grandmamma. 'I understood you were an author.'

'No, dear,' said Naomi, 'not an author. Mr Dabney is an editor. He edits a very interesting weekly paper, *The Balance*. He stimulates others to write.'

'I never heard of the paper,' said Grandmamma, who is too old to have any pity.

'I must show it to you,' said Naomi. 'Frank writes for it.'

'Very well,' said Grandmamma. 'But I am disappointed. I thought that Mr Dabney wrote books. The papers are growing steadily worse, and more unfit for general reading, especially in August. I hope,' she said, turning to Mr Dabney again, 'you don't write any of those terrible letters in August about home life?'

Mr Dabney said that he didn't, and Grandmamma began to soften. 'I am very fond of literary society,' she said. 'It is one of my great griefs that there is so little literary society in Ludlow. You are too young, of course, Mr Dabney, but I am sure it will interest you to know that I knew personally both Mr Dickens and Mr Thackeray.'

Here a shudder ran round the table, and Lionel practically disappeared into his plate. I stole a glance at Mr Dabney's face. Drops of perspiration were beginning to break out on his forehead.

'Mr Dickens,' the old lady continued remorselessly, and all unconscious of the devastation she was causing, even at the sideboard, usually a stronghold of discreet impassivity, 'Mr Dickens I met at an hotel in Manchester in the 'sixties. I was there with me dear husband on business, and we breakfasted at the same table. Mr Dickens was all nerves and fun. The toast was not good, and I remember he compared it in his inimitable way to sawdust.'

Mr Dabney ate feverishly.

'I remember also that he made a capital joke as he was giving the waiter a tip, a me dear husband always used to call a douceur. "There," he said—.'

Mr Dabney twisted a silver fork into the shape of a hairpin.

It was, of course, Naomi who came to the rescuer. 'Grand mamma,' she said, 'we have a great surprise for you—the first dish of strawberries.'

'So early!' said the old lady. 'How very extravagant of you, but how very pleasant.' She took one and ate it slowly, while Mr Dabney laid the ruined fork aside and assumed the expression of a reprieved assassin.

'"Doubtless",' Grandmamma quoted, '"God could have made a better berry, but doubtless He never did." Do you know,' she asked Mr Dabney, 'who said that? It was a favourite quotation of me fawther's.'

'Oh, yes,' said Mr Dabney, who had been cutting it out of articles every June for years, 'it was Bishop Butler.'

The situation was saved, for Grandmamma talked exclusively of fruit for the rest of the meal. Ludlow, it seems, has some very beautiful gardens, especially Dr Sworder's, which is famous for its figs. A southern aspect.

At one moment, however, we all went cold again, for Lionel,

who is merciless, suddenly asked in a silence, 'Didn't you once meet Thackeray, Grandmamma?'

Naomi, however, was too quick for him, and before the old lady could begin she had signalled to her mother to lead the way to the drawing-room.

The Faith Cure

By A.G. Shirreff

    Dragging on a pair of crutches his emaciated frame,
    To the Pir at Pipra ferry Ahmaq the Julaha came.
    'Holy Saint,' he cried, 'have pity, and exert thy power to save
    One whom magic arts are hurrying prematurely to the grave.
    As you know, the Tharu women all possess the evil eye,
    And its pitiable victims are most often such as I.
    For these witches have a weakness for a handsome bachelor
    Such as I was only lately—such as I shall be no more.
    There's a fatal fascination in the Tharu woman's glance;
    If she once has overlooked you, you don't stand an earthly chance.
    There's a buxom Tharu widow who sells fish in Tulsipur;
    She has cast the glamour on me, I am absolutely sure.
    See, my limbs are all a-tremble, and my skin is ashen grey;
    All my strength is turned to water; I am withering away.
    These are symptoms of the Lohna, which invariably ends
    In excruciating torments, as I hear from all my friends.
    Soon my liver, being shrivelled to the bigness of a pea,
    Will be riven from my midriff, which will be the end of me.
    Be the end? I wish it were, though. After death I shall be still

Everlastingly the victim of that wicked woman's will.
I shall flitter at the midnight through the glimmering forest
    glades,
Speeding on her gruesome errands in a troop of gibbering
    shades.
It is you alone can save me from this miserable fate.
Holy father, have compassion; help me ere it be too late.
'Yes,' the sage said, 'I can heal you, if my bidding you obey.
Tell me first, how came you hither, and on which side of
    the way?'
Ahmaq wondered at the question. 'I arrived here,' he replied,
    'With the aid of these two crutches, keeping to the
    left hand side.'
'This then,' said the sage, 'will cure you. Go straight back
    to your abode,
Walking only on the pattri on the right side of the road.'
'Is that all?' said the Julaha. 'That is all,' replied the Pir.
'One thing more, though—those two crutches. You had
    better leave them here.'
Ahmaq did so and departed, crawling painfully and slow,
But he felt a vast improvement after half a mile or so.
By the time he passed Turkaulia health was glowing in
    his cheeks;
And he reached his home an-hungered as he had not been
    for weeks.
With a day or two's high feeding when his tone was quite
    restored,
Back he journeyed with a present of the best he could afford.
'Twas a web of his own weaving worked upon a special
    plan,
All the colours of the rainbow rioting in every span.

When the gift had been accepted, Ahmaq said, 'If there is nought
Unbefitting in the question, tell me how the cure was wrought.'

Said the sage, "Tis very simple. As you journey back today,
You will notice there are nim-trees on the right side of the way.
That the nim has healing virtue you no doubt already know.
To that virtue's efficacy your recovery you owe.'
Back went Ahmaq, and thenceforward night and day his constant theme
Was the wisdom of the hermit, and virtue of the nim.
But the holy man's disciple, as the patient went away,
Said, 'With your permission, Master, there is some-thing I would say.
If he journeyed on the left side when from Tulsipur he came,
And returned upon the right side, either way it was the same.
Either way it was the same, and there's no reason on this showing,
Why the nim-trees should have cured him not in coming but in going.'

Then the sage of Pipra ferry answered smiling—and I think—
That he must have winked, if ever holy sages deign to wink—
'Yes, I nearly made a blunder; but the risk was very slight. Was there ever a Julaha knew his left hand from his right?
For the nim-tree's power to cure him,—you may doubt it if you will;
It is every whit as true as Tharu magic's power to kill.'

The Abbot, at the story's end,
Said, 'I approve your moral, friend.
Many folk's troubles would be less
Could they be brought to understand
That oft they cause their own distress,
And hold its cure in their own hand.'
More had he said in the same strain,
But now the Thakur sang again.

Can you blame for what is written on your forehead anyone?
If the owl is blind by daylight would you criticise the sun?
Would you criticize the sun if aloes bloom not every spring,
Or the cloud if raindrops fall not in the bottle's opening? Thus
says Girdhar, prince of poets, if your efforts miss their aim,
Blame yourself, or blame your fortunes; whom else can you
justly blame?

> First published in *The Canning College Magazine*,
> Lucknow, 1917

A Comedy in Capricorn

By Morley Roberts

It was in her aunt's box at the Opera that Gwendolen Oakhurst first met Lord Bampton. They were playing something revolutionary by Stravinsky, but to Gwen the music was but a prelude to her own romance.

'He's certainly handsome,' said Gwen pensively, as she looked across the theatre.

'And wishes to meet you, my dear,' said old Lady Mary Warrington. 'With a reserved nature like Harry's, that speaks whole encyclopaedias.'

'"Tell me about him,' said Gwen. 'I really think I shall like him, Auntie.'

'Like him? You will love him, my dear,' dear Lady Mary. 'He has looks, brains, immense wealth, and is of the kindliest disposition. With such advantages, one expects to find a failure somewhere, perhaps in manners. His are perfect. He possesses the magnificent calm which was held in my youth to distinguish the well bred.'

'Has he no faults whatever?' asked her niece.

'If he was one, it is a virtue,' replied Lady Mary, 'and one which should be an addition to you. He adores animals to a degree beyond reason. He even breeds wild horses in his park, and he asks to be introduced to you! Do you want an archangel?'

'With wings?' asked Gwen. 'Not with my passion for china!'
'I have none on my visiting list,' said Lady Mary.

On one whose heart was also warm, who adored animals and was herself a notably sweet example of the type best represented by Gainsborough in his most successful portraits, such representations could not fail to have an instant effect, although Lady Mary's collocation of wild-horse breeding and a desire for an introduction was somewhat startling. When representation was replaced by adoring reality, the result was all that Lady Mary hoped for. It came about with such amazing rapidity that in less than a week there would have been news concerning his daughter to be imparted to Colonel Oakhurst had not Gwen begged her lover to give her time to break it. She owned that her father was conservative to an extreme degree, and that any change whatsoever was apt to disturb him, and possibly the neighbourhood, since long employment in India had given him the high military complexion and habit which betoken irascibility

'As long as our marriage is not delayed,' said Lord Bampton amiably, 'I do not mind postponing the news of our engagement. I will, then, call early next week and ask for permission to pay you my addresses, dearest.'

'They will be well received,' said Gwen, smiling.

'And if your dear, ferocious, white-haired father is not amenable, I shall, of course, run away with you,' said her lover, as he kissed her hand.

'With your wild horses, Harry?' asked Gwendolen.

'They would symbolise my feeling,' said Lord Bampton. 'But I am very happy.'

And so was Gwen, though she was a little nervous when her

lover called at Warrington Grange a few days later. Even Mrs Oakhurst did not know how far matters had really advanced, but the colonel showed no irascibility when she hinted, not vaguely, that his daughter had made a more than notable conquest. It is true that he searched his mind for objections in order to relieve his conservative conscience, but he owned presently that he had heard nothing against his would-be son-in-law save that he was, perhaps, somewhat eccentric in his devotion to the animal kingdom.

'Still, that's nothing, and if he don't shoot or hunt it can't be helped. It's his loss, not mine,' said the colonel. 'I don't care a Continental! He may come here with his wild horses if he likes, or with a chimpanzee! Didn't I hear he keeps 'em?'

'Will he really bring one with him?' asked Mrs Oakhurst anxiously. 'I don't think quite I should care for a chimpanzee to come here. The animal might break something.'

'Let him bring a gorilla if he likes and break up the house,' said the colonel, chuckling. 'I'll tell Benson that if Lord Bampton turns up with a polar bear or a Bengal tiger it's to come into the drawing-room. For I'll say this much: that, on thinking it over, my dear, there's not a man in England I'd prefer for a son-in law. I remember Dicky Brown, who knows everyone on earth, sayin' Bampton had the manners of Lord Chesterfield and the morals of the Archbishop of Canterbury, while as for property he owns half this county and a coal-mine in Yorkshire. If he brings the Zoo, you'll see me take it like a lamb! By the Lord Harry, like a lamb!'

Long years in India had made the colonel look like anything but a lamb. And when he gave orders they were not neglected. He feared no one but his wife and his Scotch gardener; and Benson, the butler, in spite of his imposing appearance, was but as clay in his hands.

'Look here, Benson,' said the colonel, 'Lord Bampton will call this afternoon about four.'

'Yes, sir,' said the butler.

'If everything isn't spick and span and as bright as blazes there will be appointments vacant in this infernal neighbourhood,' cried the colonel fiercely. 'And if that damned Thompson drops the tea-tray again I'll drag him out into the garden and cut his throat from ear to ear.'

'I will attend to everything myself, sir,' said Benson.

'And another thing,' said the colonel; 'his lordship is fond of pets.'

'Yes, sir?' said the butler.

'And I understand he takes them about with him,' said the colonel. 'So if he brings a chimpanzee or a gorilla with him it's to come into the drawing-room; right in, by all that's holy!'

'How shall I know if it's a chimpanzee or a gorilla, sir?' asked the butler.

'By its bite, of course,' repied the colonel. 'But when I say a chimpanzee or a gorilla, I mean any livin' thing, a polar bear or a Bengal tiger or billy-goat. Do you understand clearly-quite, clearly?'

'Quite clearly, sir,' said the butler, who by now was prepared to usher into the drawing-room any animal whatsoever, even if it were an elephant or a crocodile.

'I'm to know it by its bite, am I?' he said bitterly. 'At times there's no knowin' what to make of the colonel. He's the most harbitrary gent in the county.'

It was about a quarter to four when his lordship's car, driven unostentatiously by himself, stayed outside the imposing front entrance of Warrington Grange. By one of those highly remarkable coincidences which seem to happen in order to bring the pure, logical sequence of the universe into contempt, a handsome young billy-goat, about three parts grown, and that very day imported into the village by the blacksmith, had broken loose from its tether and wandered into the colonel's grounds. Finding rich feed there, he had satiated his appetite, and was now resolved to satisfy the curiosity which seems inherent in the species. Having been brought up by hand, he was of an amiable and kindly disposition, and well disposed towards humanity. It may be, of course, that Lord Bampton's fondness for pets of all kinds was by some mysterious means communicated to the goat, for the lively animal rushed from behind the car just as Lord Bampton alighted. The genial creature, pleased to be with company after a period of solitude, uttered a friendly *baa* as he mounted the steps side by side with the expected and honoured guest. At that very moment Benson appeared at the door, and Lord Bampton was ushered into the drawing-room with the goat following him. The butler, being much relieved to find that he was under no necessity to recognize the species of this unlikely per by its bite, considered himself peculiarly fortunate in finding it not only gentle but tractable, and so much attached to its master that it entered the room without being coerced or chased into doing so.

Colonel Oakhurst was alone in the drawing-room when the curious pair entered. Mrs Oakhurst considered it advisable to leave them alone for a while in order that Lord Bampton might be at full liberty to speak to Gwendolen's father. She and Gwen therefore waited a while in the library.

'I am delighted to meet you, Lord Bampton,' said Colonel Oakhurst, 'and as my wife and daughter are for the moment not here, you must allow me to introduce myself.'

It seemed obvious to Lord Bampton that he and Colonel Oakhurst would be friends. For in order to please his guest the colonel patted the goat, even while he wondered at his choice of pets, and the visitor was obviously touched by the affection displayed by its owner for this highly engaging animal. As the goat wandered round the room with all the curiousity owned to be characteristic of the race, host and guest alike expatiated upon its merits. It ate part of a cushion tassel, and though the colonel cursed it in his heart he smiled with what seemed ferocious tenderness.

'It's a very fine goat,' said Lord Bampton. 'Very fine indeed.'

'Yes, a splendid animal—splendid. I—I love goats,' sputtered the colonel. 'It's well bred, too—dashed well bred.'

The splendid well-bred goat sampled another sofa-cushion, and Lord Bampton could not help wondering at the splendid well-bred calm of his host. For, judging merely by his complexion and his fierce white moustache, he would have thought him rather more explosive than dynamite. It was odd that Gwen had not mentioned her father's passion for pets.

'I understand you have an uncommon love for animals,' said the colonel.

'I grieve that it is uncommon,' said Lord Bampton, fervently following the line of agreement indicated. 'I adore them, as you do!'

'You don't draw the line anywhere?' asked the colonel, as the goat climbed the sofa and eyed a shining bureau which stood close by.

'Absolutely nowhere,' said Lord Bampton, wondering if his host did.

'Have you many pets of this kind?' 'Oh, yes; I have a most delightful pet lamb.' 'Is it at all mischievous?' asked the colonel.

'At times,' said Lord Bampton; 'but, like you, I love to see animals happy and active.'

The happy and active goat made a wonderful spring and landed safely on the bureau.

'How beautifully he jumps!' cried the colonel, wishing he could boil the animal in a brass pan.

'Magnificently,' said Lord Bampton, thinking his host must be mad to allow a goat in such a beautiful room. 'but won't he break something?'

'It doesn't matter if he does,' said the colonel, looking at the goat as if he were hypnotized. 'I rather want something broken.'

'You do? Isn't that china good?'

'Not if the goat likes to break it,' said the colonel. This room has been just the same for the last hundred years, and I'm tired of it—fairly wearied out by it.'

The goat, after balancing himself in the most beautiful manner, jumped from the bureau upon a table, and only dislodged an old punch-bowl.

'He certainly jumps very skilfully,' said Lord Bampton. 'I thought he might bring everything down. How he does enjoy himself!'

'True!' said the colonel. 'It affords me the deepest, the most enchanting pleasure to see animals enjoy themselves. Some don't! Some men hate to! I absolutely know men who would cut that goat's throat, or boil it or fry it!'

'Do you really?' asked Lord Bampton, with surprise. 'There is no end to human cruelty. I have rarely seen a goat who could jump better. You don't mind him chewing that curtain?'

'Not in the least,' said Colonel Oakhurst. 'It's old brocade very old, too old! Let him do as he likes.'

'You almost excel me in your love of animals,' said Lord

Bampton warmly; 'but there is, I maintain, no sign of an amiable nature so certain. I try all my friends by that test. This particular goat is really a most remarkable animal, and seems to have immense intellectual curiosity.'

'It looks like it,' growled the colonel. 'Now just you watch him! He's going to jump on that table.'

'It looks a highly polished and very slippery table,' said his guest; 'will he be able to keep his footing? I am curious to see.'

The goat made a spring and, landing on the table, slid with all four feet together, and only brought up on the edge.

'He seems to have scratched the polished surface,' said Lord Bampton. 'Do you mind his scratching it?'

'Oh, no, not in the least,' said the colonel, with powerfully concentrated calm. 'The table belonged to my great-grandfather, and it's high time it was scratched. Till now there wasn't a scratch on it.'

'Does Mrs Oakhurst like goats?' asked Lord Bampton. The colonel chewed at his lips and made curious sounds.

'Oh, yes, she has a perfect passion for them! But being, as most women are, a trifle uncertain in her temper, she is apt to take a dislike to a particular goat.'

'Surely not to this very delightful animal?' asked the courteous guest, with an air of warm, interested surprise at the bare possibility.

'What, dislike a goat like that?' roared the colonel. 'Such an active, inquiring animal! Oh, no! Why, if it was a simple, dull, inactive goat she would sell it and buy another just like that!'

The goat immediately demonstrated that it was not dull or inactive by springing form the hitherto unscratched table that had belonged to the colonel's great-grandfather to one which had belonged to his grandmother, and brought a large silver bowl with a crash to the ground, as he and the table cover and the bowl slid off together. With beautiful agility, the goat avoided damage to himself and, making a pleasing little buck, began to eat some flowers from the bowl and drink a little of the water as it meandered over the parquet floor.

'And Miss Oakhurst?' asked Lord Bampton, wondering what he should do when they were married if Gwen introduced goats into the drawing-room of Woodhurst.

'She also likes 'em!' gasped the colonel, wondering if a rich and noble son-in-law were worth the price he was paying.

'Does she feel towards them as you do?'

'Oh, no!' said the colonel. 'Oh, no; I absolutely defy her to come up to the feelings with which I regard this goat! She couldn't—couldn't do it! My feelings with regard to this goat are indescribable—perfectly indescribable!'

'They do you honour,' said Lord Bampton.

The goat now inspected an old Venetian mirror, and, discovering a rival in it, after a few preliminary bucks, rose up and charged the other goat which so obviously intended to charge him. There was a fearful crash, and after a moment's surprise at his sudden victory, the successful warrior sought other fields.

'I'm afraid he's broken that mirror,' said Lord Bompton.

'It's time it was broken—full time,' said the colonel desperately. 'It's—it's only an old Venetian thing an ancestor of mine brought to England. I'll order a nice new one from Tottenham Court Road.'

It was certainly remarkable that such a man should speak like that of an old Venetian mirror; but as Lord Bampton knew those who owned goats became mad so far as goats were concerned, a very common observation among those who kept other animals and went insane in other ways, he felt he could say nothing. The colonel also felt for the moment that he could say nothing. A determination of blood to the head seemed to threaten him with apoplexy, and he was perfectly aware that his complexion was that of a ripe prize tomato as his hands shook with the madly repressed desire to strangle Lord Bampton's goat without delay. To save his own life and that of this accursed animal it was necessary for him to quit the room at all costs. He choked as he said he must leave his guest for a moment.

'I'll see if my wife and daughter have got back,' he sputtered. 'You don't mind if I leave you and the goat for a minute?'

'Not at all,' said Lord Bampton; 'we shall no doubt enjoy ourselves while you are away.'

And even as the colonel hastened blindly to the door, the goat obviously took a fancy to something upon the mantelpiece. It was perhaps a piece of old Chelsea, or the photograph of the colonel in a silver frame. The animal was not at all awed by the difficult approach to his desire, and Lord Bampton watched him with great curiosity, being firmly convinced it was not the first time the animal had been up there. By a very skilful use of a sofa, an occasional table, and the back of an easy chair, Billy achieved his desire, and stood with all four feet together on the summit of his Matterhorn, having done nothing more in the way of damage then upsetting the little table and knocking a leg off it, and capsizing a brass tray into the fender.

'Bravo, Billy!' said his lordship, and Billy baaed.

And so did the colonel in the passage—for he ran against his wife and Gwendolen.

'How—how do you like him?' they asked eagerly.

It was then that the colonel baaed and made strange and peculiar noises.

Mrs Oakhurst and Gwendolen took him by the arms. He seemed in the first throes of an epileptic fit.

'What is it? Oh, what is it?' they cried in chorus.

'That—that accursed Bampton!' said the colonel. 'He's wreckin' the house—fairly wreckin it!'

'Oh, father,' said Gwen, 'what *can* you mean? Do—do be calm!'

'Ain't I calm?' roared the colonel, as he tugged at his collar. 'I'm so calm it's killin' me. The goat, the goat!'

'Tom, what goat are you speaking of?' asked his wife. 'Tell us—do tell us!'

'Lord Bampton's goat, his pet goat, that he brought with him,' gasped the colonel. 'He says it's splendid, well-bred goat with amazin' intellectual curiosity, and, by the Holy Poker, if you want real cold-blooded calmness go in and see his infernal well-bred lordship fairly eggin' on the animal to do more damage. I think he must be mad, for there's nothing left—nothing! The room's a wreck and so am I, and every time it smashed something he smiled and said it was a well-bred goat, or a fine goat, or that it jumped beautifully, and I—What did I do—why I said, curse me, that it was a damned well-bred goat, when the infernal beast was wrecking my house, and that it was a very, very fine goat, oh, Lord, and that it jumped, oh, so beautifully! Go in and see for yourselves. There, listen!'

And what they heard was the fall of the brass tray.

'Why, the infernal thing must be on the mantelpiece, or perhaps his mad master is,' gurgled the colonel. 'Look here, Mary, I can't stand this I can't!'

And the unhappy old gentleman took several short runs

up and down the passage.

'There must be some mistake—' began his wife.

'Go in, go in and see!' sputtered the colonel. 'Let me stay here. I'll put my head under the tap in the bathroom and come back presently.'

And he took a longer run for the bathroom.

'What shall we do?' asked Gwendolen's mother. 'You said he was everything a man should be.'

'And so he is,' said Gwen firmly. 'I don't care if he does keep goats. I'll cure him of that later. Whatever happens, you must keep calm. Come in, or I'll go by myself.'

Thus encouraged, Mrs Oakhurst entered the drawing-room and nothing but the sense of nobles se oblige kept her from uttering wild yells worthy of an East End lady when the cat breaks ornaments in the parlour. For upon the mantelpiece, the lambrequin of which she had embroidered with her own hands, the goat was now disporting himself. At every step something came into the fender, and at every crash the goat was more and more pleased with himself. It seemed also that he pleased Lord Bampton, who did not observe the ladies come in.

'Bravo, Billy!' said his lordship.

'Baa,' said Billy.

'You're simply magnificent, Billy,' said his lordship, 'and the most remarkable goat I ever saw.'

By this time Mrs Oakhurst has recovered herself. The damage was done and could not be undone. But the possible match remained. That his lordship had desired to meet Gwendolen was much, but Lord Bampton, whose manners, if eccentric in points, were irreproachable, was said never to forgive want of manners in others. It suddenly occurred to her that it might even be that he had determined to put the Oakhursts to a severe test—the very severest he could devise. If that was so, she and Gwen, to whom she whispered her conclusions as Billy upset the other brass tray, would not fail to meet the occasion, whatever stress was put upon them.

'Good afternoon, Lord Bampton,' said Mrs Oakhurst. And when his lordship turned and saw not only Gwendolen, but her mother as well, taking matters so sweetly, he was doubly impressed, once by the fact of their high-bred calm and again by the certainty that nothing but a series of similar dramas conducted on many other occasions by Colonel Oakhurst could possibly account for it.

'As my husband is detained for a moment, my daughter must introduce us,' said Mrs Oakhurst.

The beautiful calm courtesy and deep interest shown by Lord Bampton as he was made aquainted personally with Gwendolen's mother assured them that his manners were perfect, while this fact was confirmed by his total indifference to the noise made by his curious pet.

As was only natural, the conversation turned cheerfully and lightly upon goats in general, and particularly upon the goat in the room.

'The goat really seems to be enjoying himself today,' said Mrs Oakhurst, settling herself in a settee from which she had an admirable view of the Matterhorn and the goat upon its dangerous traverse.

'Colonel Oakhurst made the very same remark,' said Lord Bampton. 'It is delightful to find you are all so fond of animals.'

'I told you I adored them,' said Gwendolen, smiling.

'Do you like goats as much as your father does' asked his lordship.

'Even more,' said Gwendolen truthfully.

Lord Bampton allowed himself the trifling relaxation of a look of mild wonder.

'Dear me, you don't say so,' he remarked. 'Still, they have a peculiar elegance of their own, and it does not really surprise me. I can forgive anyone anything who is fond of animals. I think, by the way, that the one on the mantelpiece is measuring with his eye the distance from his perch to your settee, Mrs Oakhurst.'

But before he or Mrs Oakhurst could move, the goat launched himself into the air and missing her head by some inches, landed on the bare barquer floor and slid for ten feet, thus well displaying the peculiar elegance for which his lordship commended the goat family. Mrs Oakhurst, although it was the first time in her life that a goat had jumped over her from a mantelpiece, once more displayed the high-bred calm which had pleased their guest. It now led him on to the further reflection that, if her mother was thus attuned to the peculiar harmonies of the colonel's mind, and preserved the Horatian precept of keeping cool when in difficulties, her daughter was likely to make an equally good wife. Thus every action of the goat and Mrs Oakhurst and Gwendolen riveted the fetters of love upon Lord Bampton. He naturally assumed that their passion for the animal would make them interested in a light zoological sketch of the *Capra bircus* or Domestic Goat, and of the *Capra aegagrus*, the wild goat or *paseng* of the Persians.

'The *paseng* ranges from the Himalayas to the Caucasus,' he told them, and they well believed it, for the goat, having left the Himalayas of the mantelpiece, discovered Caucasus in the grand piano, and, perhaps imagining that a pile of modern music represented Elburz, leapt upon the piano lightly. The sound that proceeded from it seemed to excite his curiosity, for he stamped as though trying the instrument's general resonance, and then climbed on the peak of music.

'You don't mind him being on the piano, I trust?' said Lord Bampton, breaking off in his description of the reasons why the sacrifice of the goat to Athena was forbidden on the Acropolis, just at the point that Mrs Oakhurst longed for him to give a practical example in the art of sacrifice to the goddess of domestic order.

'Certainly not,' said Gwen, 'if it pleases the goat.'

'He seems to take great interest in the music,' said Lord Bampton.

'He may eat a great deal of Debussy without getting much further,' said Gwen, as she saw the animal devouring 'Li'Apres-midi d'un Faune'.

And while the goat browsed like a destructive critic among modern music, the incipient lovers and Mrs Oakhurst discussed Stravinsky, Tcherepnine, and Strauss. The conversation was, however, interrupted by the goat discovering that the keyboard suggested to his native instincts a snowy and rocky mountain path. He leapt upon it, and was so greatly surprised by the result that he left it with a wild buck and landed with a clatter among the fire-irons.

'That last simple chord that he struck distinctly reminded me of a theme of Moussorgsky's,' said Lord Bampton. 'But, see! His interest in the instrument is by no means exhausted.'

Certainly the goat had both courage and curiosity, for after refreshing himself with a bite of Tschaikowsky and a taste of Brahms he returned to the instrument and walked up and down the keyboard with the greatest delight. His lordship pointed out how evident it was that the goat was pleased with the simple wood-notes which he evoked, and from this built up a pleasing theory as to the origin of much modern music. Gwendolen argued the point eagerly, for she adored the moderns, and Lord Bampton at last admitted that it was only his fun to decry them.

'One cannot deny that there is a simple wildness in the goat's performance which is distinctly pleasing. He has, as the critics say, an idiom of his own, not remotely like the Russian idiom.'

'I think it would please my husband,' said Mrs Oakhurst thoughtfully.

'Then he likes music?' asked Lord Bampton eagerly.

'No, I cannot say that. What he likes is the simpler noises of the popular song,' replied Mrs Oakhurst. 'But I wonder what detains him. Gwendolen, please see if your father is still manipulating that cold-water tap in the bathroom.'

'Yes, mother,' said Gwendolen.

'Has the water supply gone wrong?' asked Lord Bampton as the door closed.

'Oh, no,' replied his hostess; 'but when he gets excited about anything my husband puts his head under the tap, and he is apt to leave the water running.'

'Has he been at all excited this morning?' asked his lordship. 'Has anything occurred to disturb him?'

Once more the goat played an accompaniment to the conversation, but, with no more than a casual glance at the performer, Mrs Oakhurst replied that the colonel was not disturbed but excited by the surprising activity of the goat.

'Then I gather that you have never had a goat in here before!' asked Lord Bampton.

'Not that I remember,' said Mrs Oakhurst; 'but you must not for a moment, one single moment, imagine that I object. I adore all animals, and so does Gwendolen.'

What Lord Bampton said then was a proof of his real

passion, for, during one terrible moment, he feared it was obscuring his discretion. The behaviour of Colonel Oakhurst in allowing valuable and beautiful things to be destroyed by a goat, so distinctly out of place in a drawing-room, could possibly be understood. A wild military experience might account for much. But when Mrs Oakhurst, and Gwendolen as well, displayed neither distress nor anxiety, even when the animal became musical, it opened to the lover the awful possibility of the whole household being alike afflicted. And yet it could not be! In town, Gwen had spoken as if her father was capable on occasions of going directly contrary to all dictates of reason. And was this not common in fathers, to say nothing of men generally? Lord Bampton accordingly put hesitation aside and seized the happy moment.

'You may have heard it stated that I am somewhat eccentric—'

'Oh, no,' said Mrs Oakhurst. 'I cannot credit that!'

'I have known it said,' declared Lord Bampton. 'But I am only simple and direct. I shall be so now. I wish to be allowed to pay my addresses to your daughter. One moment, I beg! In London I admired her beauty and the eager interest she shared with me in music, but since observing in her whole family such a delightful sympathy with the animal kingdom, I own I am entirely conquered. May I reckon upon your assistance and that of Colonel Oakhurst in the achievement of my dearest wishes?'

And while Mrs Oakhurst was expressing her sincere pleasure at the prospect, Gwendolen was arguing with her outraged father.

'By God, the man's mad!' said the colonel, as he rubbed his head with a rough towel. 'Mad, mad as ten thousand hatters!'

'No, dad, he is only a little eccentric,' urged his daughter.

'And mother says she thinks he has done it to try us.' 'To find out if we really love animals,' said Gwen eagerly.

'You go in and tell him I don't,' piped the colonel furiously. 'Tell him I loathe 'em, and that the only use I have for a pet is to boil it. If I thought—but no, it's impossible, impossible! By the—the—the—I'd murder him if I thought so! To try us! Oh, Lord, to try us!'

Gwen caught him by the arm.

'Do, do be patient, dearest. He's really such a dear. See how sweetly calm he is through it all.'

The colonel grasped Gwen by her arm in his turn and spoke with deadly earnestness and great rapidity.

'Look here, I'm your poor old father, and I like to behave decently, but if you talk like that you'll—you'll drive me mad. D'ye want me to have apoplexy? Calm through it all! My Venetian mirror! My great grandfather's table and a goat! Tell him I won't stand it I won't! Don't you see I can't? Calm, is he? Would he be calm if I visited his house with an unbroken jackass?'

'Oh, father, but this is only a sweet little goat,' urged Gwen. 'He is really a duck.'

'No,' said the colonel. 'I may be mad, and Lord Bampton may be madder, but I'm not so mad as to think a goat is a duck. You ain't thinking of marryin' him after this, Gwen?'

'Oh, yes, I am,' said Gwen.

'Don't,' said her father, 'don't! I beg you not to. I knew a man who liked animals so that he used to take a bag of rats into his wife's bedroom, and with 'em three terriers, and said he'd divorce her because she didn't like it. A man that will bring a goat into an inoffensive stranger's house would put rattlesnakes into a baby's cradle. What's your mother doin'?'

'She's so calm, so sweet,' said Gwen. 'Do, do be patient, father dear, and it will all come right. Please come back now. If you don't, he'll think you didn't like him! Oh, even when the goat jumped over mother's head she never turned a hair! She—she was quite majestic!'

'Was she now?' asked the colonel, as he threw the towel into the corner. 'She was majestic! And am I to be majestic too?'

'Yes,' said Gwen; 'do, do try!'

'Very well,' said her father, in sudden gloom. 'Come in and see me tryin'. But if this infernal nobleman tries it again with any other animal, a bull-caff or an orang-utan, I'll shoot it in the drawing-room. Yes, by all that's sacred, I'll blow its bleatin' head off! But come! I want to look at your mother being majestic. Majestic! Oh, Lord!'

They were just in time to see Mrs Oakhurst trying to be majestic and making very little of it. Although she sustained the conversation with serious sweetness during the absence of her husband and daughter, it was, as she owned later, a very considerable strain on her not to turn round when the goat broke the three lower glass doors of an eighteenth-century bookcase while she discoursed to Lord Bampton about Gwen and the pictures in the room. It seemed that he had a true connoisseur's appreciation of Bonington and Cotman, and found the examples of these artists work in the colonel's possession of the highest merit. But when Mrs Oakhurst left her seat to point out a drawing attributed to Turner, the goat, having finished his work among the books, made three successive bucks and charged the mistress of the house from behind.

'Majestic!' said the colonel. 'That's your word, Gwen!' 'Oh!' cried Mrs Oakhurst. 'Oh!'

'I trust most sincerely you were not hurt,' said Lord

Bampton, saving her from a fall.

'No, not in the least,' said Mrs Oakhurst, gasping, but recovering herself with great rapidity. 'I don't suppose the dear creature meant any harm. It's only his play.'

'That's it,' said the colonel thickly. 'By all that's holy, he has been playing with my bookcase! The whole room looks majestic.'

'Does it?' asked Lord Bampton. 'Does it? Ah, I see! You mean it looks like a ruin.'

'That's it,' said the colonel, throwing himself into a chair. 'I've never seen a room like this since I was in an earthquake in Chile. It wasn't any common earthquake, I tell you.'

'Earthquakes are very interesting phenomena,' said Lord Bampton. 'I too was in one once.'

'But it didn't disturb you, I'm sure,' said the colonel. 'I'll bet the unwrecked part of this house you were as cool as a ton of cucumbers.'

'I was not disturbed in the least,' replied Lord Bampton. 'I took notes and sketches.'

'Have you a notebook about you now?' asked the owner of the scene of desolation.

It seemed that Lord Bampton had none, and any further suggestion on the part of the colonel as to a sketch was stayed by the goat assaulting the window.

'He seemed to wish to go into the garden,' said the guest. 'Perhaps it might be as well to let him out.'

'It's a very fine garden,' said the colonel, 'and in perfect order, quite perfect. That's my beastly gardener's fault. I hate order myself. What I like is ruins—complete, majestic ruins! But my gardener doesn't. He's a very arbitrary gardener; there's no making him see reason. That goat will be a dead goat if you let him out.'

'Do I gather you would rather the goat remained here?' said Lord Bampton.

'I—I don't know,' said the colonel; 'he seems cramped here. Would you like him to look at the rest of the house?'

'That is as you please, of course,' said the guest. 'Do you usually let goats go everywhere, or do you keep them to this particular room'

'I don't keep 'em anywhere,' said the colonel, choking. 'They only come in as visitors—just as visitors.'

'Yes, only as welcome visitors,' said Mrs Oakhurst, eyeing her husband anxiously.

'Just as occasional visitors,' said Gwendolen sweetly. 'Do you allow them all over your house, Lord Bampton?'

'I beg your pardon,' said Lord Bampton. 'Do I allow goats all over my house? Oh, no, never, never! I don't in the least mind what they do elsewhere, but I draw the line there.'

The colonel jumped to his feet. 'Father!' said his daughter.

'I can't be majestic any more,' roared the colonel. 'I must speak—I must! What's more, I will. Do you mean to say, Lord Bampton, that you never allow your goat to enter your house? Do you mean to tell us that you are so damnably unkind to a precious pet like a half-grown billy-goat as never to let him wreck a room full of valuable furniture, never to climb upon the mantelpiece, never to smash a few ancient mirrors, and, most of all, never to butt a visitor from behind?'

'Certainly not,' said Lord Bampton warmly. 'I am, I may say, notoriously fond of animals, but though it affords me no inconsiderable pleasure to see others even more attached and devoted to them, the very last thing I myself should allow is a goat, however well bred, to be in any of my own rooms. What goats, or other pet animals, do in other houses is, of course, a matter of perfect indifference to me.'

'Stop!' said Colonel Oakhurst. 'Stop before I break a blood vessel. Perfect indifference! My hat!'

The colonel's agitation was now so obvious that it would have been ill-breeding on the part of the calmest nobleman in the kingdom not to notice it. Lord Bampton did notice it.

'Did I say anything particularly remarkable?' he asked, with perhaps a tinge of rebuke in his voice.

'Oh, no,' said the colonel. 'After all that's happened, what you said in the way of not carin' a Continental if I had a house over my head or not seemed like a long drink on a hot day. But, by this goat and the goats that ever reared over-end in a cabbage garden, there's nothing more to be said. It's no go. It can't be done. I won't allow it. I'd rather die first.'

'Than do what, dad?' asked Gwen.

The colonel gasped and again tugged at his collar.

'You—you know! You can't marry Lord Bampton—you can't! I won't have it. He's mad, mad, quite mad!'

Mrs Oakhurst rose in haste. Gwen made a step towards her lover, who looked the picture of well-bred amazement. After his own apparently sound doubts of the colonel's entire sanity it was strange to discover that for some peculiar reason his own was doubted.

'Oh, father!' said Gwen. 'Oh, Tom!' said his wife.

'Don't Tom me,' roared the colonel savagely. 'I forbid it—all of it. I won't have it. Mad, mad as a hatter!'

Lord Bampton now perceived that he was in an awkward situation. He therefore sought to temporize with the colonel knowing that to contradict a maniac in the acute stage was, by those best acquainted with the insane, considered both useless and dangerous. It seemed possible to the guest that he had unwittingly shown disapproval of the goat being in the drawing room. He hastened to remove this impression.

'Perhaps I was wrong in saying something which seemed to imply a lack of feeling for this delightful animal,' he said very earnestly. 'I assure you, Colonel Oakhurst, that when I said that what it did here was a matter of indifference to me, I by no means meant that I was not charmed and interested by it. I trust you will not think me inconsiderate to animals.'

Colonel Oakhurst went the colour of an oak tree in autumn. 'Look here!' he said, and then stopped to catch his breath. 'Pray continue,' said Lord Bampton.

'Take your damned goat out of my house,' roared the colonel, 'or by the Holy Poker I'll get a gun and shoot it!'

'Take *whose* goat?' asked Lord Bampton.

'Whose goat? Whose goat?' asked the colonel.

'Yes, whose'

'Yours, yours!' said the colonel.

And Lord Bampton, for the first time losing the calm which became him so well, sat down in the nearest chair with a positive thump. The goat came up to him, and his lordship absolutely glared at it.

'My—my goat?'

'Yes! Take it away—take it away quick, before I explode,' said the colonel. 'Or else I'll do your cursed pet a mischief.'

And Lord Bampton fairly collapsed.

'It's not my goat,' he said feebly. 'Oh, no, it's not mine! I never saw the awful animal before.'

'Oh!' said Mrs Oakhurst.

'Oh!' said Gwendolen, and once more the colonel did one of those peculiar little runs up and down the room which betokened a really disturbed state of mind.

'You never, never saw it before?' he asked at last in a curious choked whisper.

'Never, never!' said his lordship. 'Why, naturally enough, I thought it was yours!'

It was the colonel's turn to sit down. He did so, and opened his mouth three times before he could speak.

'Oh, you thought it mine, did you?' he asked. 'May I—may I ask if you thought I was twice as mad as a March hare?'

'The possibility never entered my head,' said Lord Bampton earnestly, 'I merely thought that your choice of a household per was uncommon and the latitude you gave it surprising.'

The colonel mopped his face. 'But—but it came in with you?' he urged. 'I saw it myself.'

'So did your butler,' replied Lord Bampton; 'but that doesn't make him my butler. If I had come in with a tiger after me, would that have made him my tiger? Of course I thought it was your goat.'

'Then—then whose goat is it?' asked the colonel fiercely. 'If Benson can't tell me, he'll be no one's butler in two shakes of a lamb's tail. Let me get at him!'

And then Gwen, who had been speechless, burst into laughter and interrupted her father at the door.

'Dad, didn't you tell poor Benson that Lord Bampton loved pets, and that if he brought one it was to come into this room?' she asked.

'You did, Tom,' said Mrs Oakhurst; 'yes, you did!'

'So I did,' said the colonel, 'so I did! But I never, never, reckoned on a goat! Look at the fiend now! He's eating my old Persian rug. Let him, what's it matter?'

But it did matter, for the goat was disappointed with green

worsted and eyed the whole party with malignancy.

'I apologize, Lord Bampton,' said the colonel, 'I apologize humbly and more than humbly. I—I—'

'Don't mention it,' said Lord Bampton. 'I have a confession to make.'

The colonel started.

'Look here, you ain't by any chance goin' to say it's your goat after all, are you? I tell you I couldn't, couldn't bear it!'

'No, Colonel Oakhurst,' said Lord Bampton. 'But you seem to know that I came here to ask permission to pay my addresses to Miss Oakhurst. I confess such a question would have been disingenuous since I have her permission to ask for her hand.'

'My—my hat!' said the colonel. 'You don't say so!'

'I do say so,' replied Lord Bampton firmly.

'Speak, Tom, speak!' said Mrs Oakhurst.

But the colonel couldn't speak. He looked round and, catching Gwen's beaming eye, saw the only thing to do. He took her hand and made a step towards Lord Bampton. But he didn't deliver the goods. The goat did that.

Ping Pong & Ruskin Bond

By Victor Banerjee[5]

You walked up a rickety old staircase, turned a shiny brass knob and passed through a creaky door into the horrors of the dentist's chamber. He was an ancient, asthmatic Parsee, forced to flee from the balmy shores of Bandra in Bombay to the more moderate Doon valley. He gazed deep into the gaping mouth of the cherubic young boy who was screaming his lungs out to drown the drone of the dreadful drill that stood grimly beside him. 'Great voice, terrible teeth!' the doctor wheezed.

Ruskin Bond was at an impressionable age, and would never forget the old wheezer's diagnostic proclamation about his singing voice. The years passed, and the cherub grew into a portly bundle of fun, a great writer of children's stories and quite understandably, a frustrated singer.

As a kindergartner in Bishop Cotton School, in Simla, he was the most angelic of all the choir boys. Dressed in frilly gowns and leading the Easter Parades, he never understood why the choir mistress, tapping his soft derriere with a Malacca cane, had whispered. 'Open your mouth wide, but do not, not

---

[5]Victor Banerjee, a well-known actor, photographer and director in the world of cinema, enjoys writing in his free time.

ever, utter a sound!' Those words had tormented him for many years, and even bothered him today.

Ruskin grew up on Gilbert and Sullivan, and the Grand Operas. He puffed his hair meticulously, like Nelson Eddy, and when alone in his room, used boot polish to look like Paul Robeson. He fumbled through adolescence doting palely on Eartha Kitt and Elizabeth Taylor, dueting dolefully with Jeanette MacDonald in his shower, and lamenting the locks that hid Veronica Lake from him.

Today, as he leans out of his window on a summer's eve and gazes into the shimmering lights of the Doon valley five thousand feet below, he benignly recollects the old dentist's chamber of horrors and wonders what went wrong. Parsees are a respected bunch, he ponders, they never lie. Almost two generations of Indians had grown up reading his books, and it made not the slightest difference to him. Woefully he looked up at a sky bathed in neons from the planes and with tremulous cheeks, and a lump in his throat, began to sing.

A mellifluous voice bemoaned its outcaste state and the sycamores sighed to the strains of 'Oh Rose Marie, I love you'. Windows slammed shut. Children dived under quilts. Grandmothers smiled.

For years, this disembodied voice, to natives on the hillside, had been associated with the spirit of Captain Young; the Irish cavalier who founded Mussoorie almost two hundred years ago. On certain nights of the year, the Captain's ghost haunted Landour, and you heard his horse gallop across the slopes of Mallangar. Not to be confused with any head-less horseman, Young sang. And that is how Ruskin has held onto his little secret, all these years. As a child in Kathiawar, he had hobnobbed with royalty, played Katisha in 'The Mikado,' and developed an intense passion for cricket, among other noble pursuits. Sometimes, squatting under the bellies of giant great danes in the royal kennels, Ruskin would snoop on the awkward dalliance of Monarchs with nubile concubines between overs, naturally! Later, kicking sand in the face of a moon rising above the dunes, he would dream of one day carrying of his beloved like the Red Shadow, upon a spectacular Arabian stallion, into an oasis of ice-creams and mixed fruits jellies. Smelly stables and kennels were not quite his cup of ovaltine. Cricket, and England, were.

His teens he spent in a damp attic on Jersey Island, humming 'Shrimp boats are coming', reminiscing on his days in Dehra, and wrote the memorable book *The Room on the Roof*. During the day, he worked for a stodgy travel agent whose knowledge of geography was limited to Marbella. Ruskin endeavoured to send their clients to exotic destinations that he conjured up from the romances he read and the Broadway musicals he spent his wages on. Naturally, he got the sack. He took his revenge when, on his last day at work, he vicariously booked an entire group travelling to Spain, into the 'Shangri La' in Tibet.

On his way back to London, across the fog-bound channel, he felt an enormous sense of relief. Leaning on the rails of the little ship that was ferrying him across, he could barely see the white cliffs of Dover when, overcome with nostalgia for the India he knew and missed, he burst into the Indian Love Call a la Nelson Eddy, 'When I'm calling yeeoooou....' Two short, and one long hoot from the chugging steamer were his orchestral accompaniment, and the rapid tread of feet on the deck sounded like the drumming hooves of Canadian Mounties on the approach. As his voice floated above the choppy waters, he felt someone grab him by the collar, lift him off his feet, and throw him into a life-boat. His good ship lollipop, had sprung a leak.

That probably explains why friends with twisted fenders, bubbling radiators and inexplicable flat tyres request him not to sing anymore, at least not while taking a ride in their cars: by that hangs another unkind tale.

Still in his early twenties, Ruskin returned to India, a celebrity. In Dehra Dun he found the old jackfruit tree in whose crevice he had put away his little treasures. His catapult, a few marbles and some silver and gold chocolate wrappers. Far from the maddening fog, he lay back on the grass composing lyrics, courting penury, and rejecting the advances of a mustachioed wench who eventually put him off marriage forever. It also did not help that the Garhwali girl he swooned over, never purred back. However, in early spring, when the tree blossomed, he came down with a severe attack of hay fever. Then, fortune struck.

An oily sanitary engineer barged into his apartment unannounced, and grinning like a slaughterable goat, stood by his bed with one filthy foot on 'Tintern Abbey' and another on the Manchester United Football scarf that Ruskin prized above everything he possessed. Ruskin turned purple. 'So you are the great Ruskin Bond, like James Bond eh?' the flatula guffawed, 'I've come to make you an offer. A hundred rupees for a slogan, a simple line, extolling the virtues of the automatic flush I've invented to go with my custom made thunder-box.

El Crudo guffawed again, and were it not for a bout of sneezing that suddenly gripped our young lyricist, the inventor would have been flushed down the stairs quicker than he had mounted them. 'May I sit?' he said, pointing to a three-legged stool, 'is it safe?' Ruskin could do no more than nod involuntarily as he glared over the drenched handkerchief he held clasped to his nostrils. Then it hit him. That was it. 'SIT SAFE!'

He paid the rent, picked up a clean shirt from the dhobi, delivered United's scarf to the dry cleaners, took an exclusive tonga drawn by a white horse to the Odeon, and bought a dress circle sent to the matinee of 'Brigadoon'. Fortune, like the Cheshire cat, smiled thereafter.

And that brings me to Ping and Pong, my two trusted roosters who fearlessly crow on my side every time my little Turandot hoists a rolling pin. Only when caught stepping on her pansies, or nibbling on the celery, are they filled with the dread that I live with. It was they who drew out the repressed talents of Bond, the baritone.

Outside my window is a peach tree on whose branches my chickens roost every afternoon. I am not too sure about metempsychosis, but I am hard pressed to explain how and why my chickens begin to sing every time they hear opera. The phenomenon has been observed by many a curious visitor, including Ruskin, who has marvelled at how the red Pong prefers Pavarotti and the speckled Ping, Domingo. The hens only chirp in when the sopranos and contraltos come in.

Early last December, I was at my desk daydreaming, and admiring the crackling patterns of frost on my window pane. My diary had said Mozart died, two hundred years ago. Nature seemed to be paying silent tribute, for all was quiet; and then I heard a voice in the orchard.

'Diess irae, dies illa...the day of wrath shall dissolve the world in ashes'. Mozart's requiem, rendered immaculately. I peered through gnarled vines and saw Ruskin. He was seated on a wrecked settee, with Ping and Pong clutched under his arms. They listened silently to the soul of a silenced lover of song. The apple tree overheard overhead, and blossomed.

The old Parsee had not lied. A great voice.

The Music Man

By *Vijay N. Shankar*

The first thing I heard the night I moved into the room under a false name—the landlord only wanted a South Indian tenant—was the saxophone. Now that was a from my old room neighbour who spent most of his time beating his wife and then making up to her. I couldn't sleep of course because the saxophone went on like a cat somebody had stepped upon. So I smoked the last of my cigarettes and then went next door to borrow one.

Joseph Samuel was a small man with a big repertoire of swear words and an abrupt manner. 'Christ in heaven,' he said at the door, 'I'm trying to create music, man.' Then his face swung into formal lines. 'Yes?' He was almost a dwarf but he squeezed my hand so hard that I stopped feeling sorry about his height.

'I'm your neighbour. Ran out of cigarettes.' 'Have you got a girlfriend in your room?' he asked. 'No.'

'Right. Because the guy before you said my saxophone distracted him from his girlfriend. I play in a band and my name is Mister Samuel.' He stepped aside for me and smiled the first time.

He had this pompous way about him which I found later was

no pose at all. It was his way of putting on a few extra inches.

'Meet my wife,' he said and I looked around the empty room.

'Sally,' he said and laughed. Then walked over to his bed and patted the gleaming saxophone. 'The best wife a man ever had, eh?'

'I'm a writer,' I said. I had practised that line so many times.

'That's why you're here in this dump, man. God bless us artist types.' He threw me his packet of cigarettes. That, as the man said, was the beginning of a beautiful friendship. Actually a ribald, drunken, cry-on-your-shoulder kind of friendship with an impossible man. You just couldn't believe that he was there. He was broke most of the time of course, but had worked out a foolproof system of redistributing loans. So if he borrowed two hundred at a certain time, he took it from four people and kept on paying back three of them while he used the money taken from only one of them.

What was most surprising was that he actually had political views of his own. 'I believe in socialism, man,' he said to me one day after reading the newspaper he borrowed every morning from me. 'It makes you feel good to know that things are going to change...that one day I'll have a house of my own.'

'You're just dreaming, Joseph.'

'That's why I voted for Mrs Gandhi's party, man. They had the best dreams to give.' I laughed at that but he was dead serious. 'You may be an angry young man, but there are millions like me who want this kind of dream. We're quite happy. And look at the music I play. A lot of dream stuff from a shining, golden world.

'Who knows that I go back with my saxophone to this dump of a room where there's no water and the stairs stink.

And the people who hear me…they go back too, to places like this…even worse. That's life and life is a bitch, as Mr Hallsworth used to say.'

'Who's that?'

'God rest his soul. He was the undertaker in whose house I lived before coming to Delhi. That was in Bombay. A great man who quoted your friend Shakespeare.'

As they say of course, behind every great and not so great man there is a woman. In Joseph's case, the woman was about ten years behind him. 'Used to sing like an angel, she did,' he said to me one cold night just before Christmas. 'Would have married her too and everything was fixed up.'

'You didn't?'

'No. She married a good-for-nothing pianist in Bombay. I don't blame her. I never was much to look at. But what I got is soul, man. That's God's own truth. Do you think I have a soul?'

For a moment I thought Joseph was going metaphysical on me and I didn't like any of it. I would have much rather heard him talk about his bacchanalias in Colombo where he had lived for some years. So to cut short any prospective argument, I agreed that he had a soul.

'Anyhow, I'm happy with Sally. I live to play this,' he fondled the keys of his saxophone.

But try as I might, I never could get him to take me along when he lumbered out with his saxophone to play it, God knows where. He left in the afternoons and came back close to midnight about ready to fall apart. 'You can hear me all you want right here,' he said when I suggested that I might go along with him. He went fishing almost every Sunday. He always left too early for me but I saw him come back wearing his faded T-shirt and trying to get his outside fishing rod in past the door and the corner just before the stairs. It was a sight as he strutted about when he caught a fish or two and showed it off to everyone in the building. Finally the fish went as a goodwill bribe to the landlord and Joseph made a great production of it as he made the formal presentation, bending over double and patting the landlord's pretty daughter as he forced them to accept the fish. 'It makes him feel very special,' he said to me when I suggested that we could eat the fish ourselves. 'A fish or two every Sunday and I don't have to pay the rent. When he's so terribly grateful to me, how can he ask for the rent? That's why it's worth buying the fish and giving it to him.'

'You mean, you don't catch them?' I asked with some surprise. 'Me catch fish,' he laughed. 'Never caught one in my life.'

Excepting for the day when Joseph really dropped a brick. He had been drinking more than usual and I thought it was just because it was Christmas eve. He went out as usual with his saxophone and large briefcase, staggering as he walked unsteadily. 'Want me to come?' I asked him and he shook his head vigorously. 'Don't be silly, man...who says I'm drunk, eh?' he said, I went back to an article I was doing. Maybe I should have taken away his quart bottle of rum before he left. That thought came later.

He came back, or rather was brought back at night by some men wearing the multi-coloured costume of a marriage band. The people who march along before the bridegroom's horse.

Joseph was in the same costume too and it took a long minute to register that he played in that kind of band. And he was far out drunk, falling on all sides as he clutched Sally and mumbled incoherently. 'He just wouldn't stop playing some silly western tune,' one of the men said, 'We were playing the latest film hits and Joseph just played this silly music.'

He had a splitting hangover next morning and was painfully contrite because we had all found out about his band. 'I had to join up with them. Everyone faces hard times,' he said. 'And I don't know why but the only thing I could play last evening was the funeral march. It came out from the soul, you know.' I handed him some coffee. 'You were playing what?'

He doubled up laughing as the irony struck him too. 'Christ, the funeral march.' The coffee fell all over him as we laughed.

But Joseph moved out the next day because everyone started calling him bandwalla. That was something he never could live down.

In Praise of the Sausage

I like a good sausage, I do;
It's a dish for the chosen and few.
Oh, for sausage and mash,
And of mustard a dash
And an egg nicely fried—maybe two?
At breakfast or lunch, or at dinner,
The sausage in always a winner;
If you want a good spread
Go for sausage on bread,
And forget all your vows to be slimmer.

Epitaph for an Escape Artiste

Here lies a famous escapologist
Who was buried on the 19th, 20th,
And then again on the 21st June.

First Kiss

I remember—I remember
The first girl that I kissed.
She closed her eyes and I closed mine,
And then—worse luck—we missed!

Last Tango in the Far Pavilions

By Bill Aitken

I've never read M M Kaye but I ran into one of her unguided tours the other weekend, a party of middle-aged English ladies on a 'Ramble of Hill Stations'. I'd been house-painting for weeks, grimly saving on the cost of labour to pay for the paint and decided I could do with a day off. I decided to walk to Everest's old bungalow beyond Mussoorie and overlooking the Yamuna as it struggles across the Doon valley. (The English ramble while we paharis prefer to straggle).

On the way I was surprised to see at a distance several ladies wearing red gym skirts with matching sunhats and knapsacks for all the world like one of those tremendously tough teams of Japanese lady climbers who give a cheery wave before they abseil off the top of Everest into the gathering gloom...to be followed shortly after by the sound of six short sharp blasts on a girl-guide whistle—the Alpine distress signal.

Later in the day on my way back I bumped into them again near a little tea-stall I always go to. They turned out to be British and disgruntled bird and wildflower watchers. They had also wanted to visit Everest's estate (they referred to him as 'Sir George' though when he lived in Mussoorie the locals called him 'Compasswala') but had lost the way.

Apparently my curiosity had been reciprocated for they admitted they had been trying to identify me through binoculars. It had to be the day I was wearing a pair of borrowed ladies ski pants with no flies. (No sex please. They're British). From the paint on my fingers, elbows and hair they deduced rightly if not accurately that I was a painter. Strange how respectable matrons perk up on meeting 'artists'. Plumbers don't have the same effect.

They were looking for a rare partridge that Dr Salim Ali had reported to be last sighted in the 1880's. I told them never mind the partridge having disappeared, the whole mountain was being systematically levelled by the limestone quarrying. To silence the environment lobby the government was 'monitoring' the destruction.

They sat gingerly on the packing cases which furnished the tea stall and intoned long, crucial instructions to my friend the Sardarji who owned the shack, on how their tea was to be prepared. Sardarji spoiled the life-and-death atmosphere by beaming to his wife—who was in control of operations and summing it all up as 'light tea'. His wife smiled back in lieu of not comprehending.

The lady Gringos were suffering not just cultural shock but aesthetic battering. The picnic spot they had been directed to was a beautiful amphitheatre of lofty deodar trailing wild roses, with bursts of rhododendron and wisteria. The municipal authorities were not satisfied with the hand of God however and had used up their allocation of cement on providing an artificial lake with cemented bottom and sides. In place of water there were painted pink and blue stripes of fluorescent brilliance. The memsahibs had been stunned into silence, shaking their heads in disbelief. It was a sight not dreamed of on land of sea or even on colour television. I'm not a snob in these matters and the PWD engineer who hit on this colour scheme, had he been born in America, might have been hailed as a master of the 'suburban primitive' school.

They had already suffered a financial trauma that Sunday morning when they learned that their hotel's licence to change traveller's cheques had expired on Saturday evening. The manager who was ignorant of the situation was grateful for them explaining their predicament and laughed uproariously at his own misfortune not realising that the British never laugh when mentioning the church, the lavatory or the bank.

Never a man to sit idle, Sardarji was fiddling with his motor cycle chain when his wife announced tea was about to be served. Reverentially the assortment of chipped china mugs of light tea arrayed on a battered tin tray was placed on a wobbling plastic topped table. It was so light it looked white. To accommodate the novel idea of 'no sugar, no milk' Sardarji's wife had added some condensed milk which is strictly neither though very much both, just in case the ladies had been jesting. Their frozen horror showed they hadn't been joking and Sardarji tried to retrieve the situation by producing a shrivelled nimbu that had wintered in his loft and attempted to squeeze it with the beatific suggestion that he was providing 'Russia tea'. Unfortunately the citric acid loosened the axle-grease on his fingers and what they got was 'Diesel cappuccino.'

My mood had already been spoiled by the unspoken resentment that I could come here regularly and tuck into two stuffed parathas visibly enjoying myself despite the fact that the Viceroy would never return. Their resentment also extended to a small party of Tibetan monks picnicking nearby. Their leader was sitting apart, stout and smiling and although a complete stranger, he seemed to be a continuation of the happy landscape, his presence perhaps accounting for the magnolia's gorgeous bloom. But he had a Polaroid camera and holy-men had no business enjoying themselves in a public place.

It seemed useless to explain that Sardarji had named his shack 'Premi Ristorent' for the ladies' quivering nostrils seemed to suspect the very air of being hostile. The whole trip appeared to have been a butter-side-down experience, even to complaining of fleas at the Mughal Agra. A very small party had come in a very big air-conditioned bus and had been put up in an empty, turreted hostelry that claimed to be the biggest of its kind in Asia. It had been chosen because inside things hadn't changed much since the British left. Tortering bearers still bore plates of cucumber sandwiches for tea, though the cucumber was actually ghia, masquerading. When I asked if they had seen the morning papers about the Falklands being invaded by a corn-beef republic all I got was a raised eyebrow and 'Really' stretched out to three syllables. It was her way of letting me know she didn't really believe that India could rise to such pleasures as the morning newspapers. Surely all the good things of life had gone back in the tin trunks of the Raj?

Literacy Lapses

A young admirer came up to James Joyce and said, 'May I kiss the hand that wrote *Ulysses*?' To which Joyce replied: 'No it did lots of other things too.'

◆

When Tennyson entered the Oxford Theatre to receive his honorary degree of Doctor of Literature, his locks hung in disorder on his shoulders, and he looked untidy and dishevelled. A voice from the gallery was heard calling out to him: 'Did your mother get your up too early, dear?'

◆

A dear old lady sitting next to P.G. Wodehouse at dinner kept raving about his work. She said she never missed reading each of his books, and that her shelves were filled with them. 'And when I tell my family,' she concluded, that I have actually been sitting at dinner with Edger Wallace, I don't know what they will say!'

Verses: From the Sanskrit

By A.G. Shirreff

1

Fondle them the first five years;
Beat them the succeeding ten:
On their cheeks when down appears,
Treat your sons as friends and men.

2

Little wise is he who wakes
Seven sleepers, which be these—
Tigers, princes, fools, and snakes,
Babies, and strange dogs, and bees.

3

Knaves and thorns two treatments suit;
All you need decide is whether
You should crush them underfoot
Or avoid them altogether.

4

Who his wealth guards jealously,
Like a wife, himself defeats;
So does he who lets it ply,
Like a woman of the streets.

5

Spend the things you chiefly cherish—
Wealth and life—to serve your friends.
Both of these must surely perish;
Let them perish for good ends.

Translations by A.G. Shirreff; from
Tales of the Sarai, 1917

When I Smelt a Rat, and Gave Up Chocolate

One of the great pleasures of life is the afternoon siesta. In Mexico and other Latin American countries, it has been perfected to a fine art. In warm countries like ours, it is almost a necessity, especially for the farmer toiling in his fields from daybreak to noon. An afternoon nap under a peepal tree or in the shade of a mighty banyan does wonders for body and soul.

I take my siesta on the same bed that I sleep upon at night, but if I am travelling, I have no difficulty in taking a nap on a plane or in a bus or in a railway waiting room, although I must admit that it's been many years since I travelled by train. Under a tree sounds romantic, but the last time I tried sleeping under a friendly horse-chestnut tree, I was woken by chestnuts falling on my head.

Bed is best, especially on a cold winter's day in the hills. And at night, a hot water bottle helps. Given a warm bed, I sleep like a baby. But like a baby, I am inclined to wake up at midnight or at one in the morning, feeling rather hungry. And for this purpose, I keep a bar of chocolate on my bedside table.

There's nothing like a chunk of chocolate in the middle of the night. It helps me feel that all's right with the world, and

I fall asleep again to dream of cricket bats made of chocolate and rainbows made of sugar candy. You must try it sometime, those of you who have difficulty in sleeping. But a few nights ago, I woke up prematurely to hear something nibbling away on my bedside table. Katr-katr, katr-katr, came the ominous sound. I switched on the bedside lamp, and there sat a fat rat, nibbling away at my chocolate!

Now I am generous with most things, and I am happy to share my chocolate with you, gentle reader, but I draw the line at rodents. So I flung a slipper at the rat, who dodged it and took off with some reluctance, and then I had to throw away the remains of the chocolate for fear of catching rat flu or something horrible.

Anyway, the next night I kept a fresh chocolate bar in a drawer of the dressing table, where I felt sure it would be safe. Once again, my dreams were interrupted by the nibble and crunch of small teeth embedding themselves in my chocolate bar. I sprang out of bed, rushed to the dressing table, pulled out the drawer, and out popped Master Rat, the champion chocolate-eater! Away he went, leaving behind only half a bar of chocolate for yours truly.

Apparently he'd found a hole in the back of the drawer, and spurred on by greed, had burrowed his way to the object of his desire.

A trap! A trap was what I needed. So I borrowed my neighbour's rat trap—not the kind that kills, but the kind that imprisons (which may be worse)—and set it up with my favorite chocolate as bait. They say rats prefer cheese, but I wasn't taking any chances.

Anyway, the trap worked, and in the morning I found a disgruntled rat staring at me through the bars of his prison like the prisoner of Zenda. Picking up the trap, I walked with it half a mile up the road, and then released Master Rat in the bushes behind a popular bakery. Very irresponsible of me, but I thought the precincts of the bakery would at least keep him occupied.

Three peaceful nights passed. Once again, I enjoyed my midnight chocolate snack.

Then—katr, katr, katr....He was back again!

'Once more into the breach, dear friends.'

Another trap was borrowed and Master Rat was jailed for a second time. And this time I was taking no chances. I engaged a taxi, drove to the Kempty waterfall with the rat in its trap, and there flung the protesting rat into the waterfall, much as the villainous Moriarty had flung poor Sherlock Homes over a certain waterfall. The last I saw of the rat, he was swimming strongly downstream towards the Yamuna bridge.

Peace at last. Chocolate forever! Dreams of candy floss and golden syrups...

And then: katr, katr, katr...

I switch on the bedside light.

Two rats are on my desk, having a tug of war with my chocolate bar.

There's only one thing to do.

I give up eating chocolates. I'll starve those rats out of existence even if, in the process, I must suffer from extreme malnutrition.

Braving Mussoorie's Madding Crowd

It's mid-season in Mussoorie and I am fighting my way down the Mall road along with thousands of tourists, holiday makers and locals, determined to enjoy the delights of the hill station. The car could make no progress, having been rammed into a pram. Fortunately the pram was empty. But as we could make better progress on foot, we abandoned the car and joined the happy throng.

Pram-pushers do good business at this time of the year as frazzled mothers soon tire of lugging their babies around on the Mall. When my royalties dry up, I shall get a pram and make a living pushing babies around. It's easier than driving a taxi.

The destination is the Savoy, where I am to lunch with Shubhadarshini, who made a TV serial called 'Ek Tha Rusty' many years ago. Since then, we have both grown older and wiser.

The crowd increases as I near Gandhi Chowk, or Library Bazaar as it is known to the locals. Here, the wayside vendors are busy, selling everything from balloons and candy-floss to boiled eggs and roasted peanuts. I am persuaded to buy a boiled egg. They even peel it for me and provide me with a generous amount of salt and pepper. The pepper gets up my nose, and

I start sneezing so vigorously that the crowd parts, making my progress easier.

After manoeuvring past the traffic jam at Gandhi Chowk, I finally reach the Savoy. Sanctuary! Its extensive grounds and garden give me a feeling of unfettered freedom. And I am welcomed like an old friend, for this was a favourite watering place in the old days.

I am welcomed to the Writers' Bar, given a gin and tonic, then led in a procession to the dining room where I am served a Shepherd's Pie, my favourite dish. The management refuses to let us pay for lunch. They are not sure if I'm real, or the returning spirit of one of those famous writers whose names are commemorated on the wall of the Writers' Bar. But I look substantial enough, more flesh than spirit, and the Shepherd's Pie finds its true home.

Two hours later, I am on the Mall again, walking a little unsteadily in the direction of home and hearth. A cycle-rickshaw is summoned. I pour myself into it, relax like an overfed sloth bear. The rickshaw barely moves, the crowd is so dense.

A large lady keeps pace with the rickshaw. She is holding a baby in her arms.

"Can you hold the baby for a little while ?' she asks, and before I can refuse, she has dumped her infant into my arms. The child does its best to remove my spectacles.

"Where are you from?' I ask the mother. 'Amritsar,' she says, 'You must come to Amritsar.'

I promise to come. When royalties run out, I can make a living as a baby-sitter in Amritsar. After some time, she takes the baby back and disappears into a beauty parlour.

Ships that pass in the night...

Finally, I arrive at the bookshop. No one is buying books

today, although some kids are looking at the colouring books on the pavement and dripping ice-cream all over them. It's a hot day and ice creams have priority over books.

Someone from the crowd recognises me, walks over and thrusts a hundred-rupee note into my hand. 'Well, thank you very much,' I say. 'That's extremely generous of you.'

"No, no !' he says. 'I want your autograph. On the note, please.'

"But is that legal?' I ask, longing to hang on to the note.

"Of course. The RBI Governor has signed it. Gandhiji's photo is on it. You have their blessings. Please sign.'

"Wouldn't you prefer an autographed book? Only sixty rupees.'

"No, I only collect notes. See, I have one autographed by John Abraham.'

Flattered to be in such starry company, I gave him my autograph. Then I bought a colouring book. Colouring it would be therapy of a sort. Better than reading gory American crime novels.

The owner of the bookstore refused to take any payment for the colouring book. Instead he suggested that I author colouring books. They sold better than books that had to be read.

And finally I stumbled home and went to bed.

Not a bad day, after all. Shepherd's Pie at the Savoy. A gin and tonic. A free colouring book. My autograph in demand — and that too, beside the RBI Governor's. And an invitation to Amritsar to be a baby-sitter.

Never a dull moment on an author's day off.

Why I Miss the Good Old GP Who Kept it Simple

Customs change with the changing times, but not always for the better.

I do miss the old GP, the family doctor, who would turn up at your house at short notice. You had only to give him a ring or send him a message saying you or one of your loved ones was down with the flu or mumps or some mysterious fever, and he'd be around in a jiffy. Years of experience enabled him to make a quick and usually accurate diagnosis and he'd write out a prescription on the spot. If he thought it was something very serious he'd direct you to the nearest hospital. If he was a good doctor, his very presence would make you feel better. He'd put his stethoscope to your chest, feel your pulse, look at your tongue, prod your tummy, and make you breathe deeply and say 'Aaah!' You took his pills religiously, and sooner or later you felt better.

Such doctors are a dying breed. Today, young doctors open smart clinics or join city hospitals, and if you want to see them you must stand in line with dozens of other patients. In spite of all the advances of medical science, sick people multiply by the day and our cities are flooded with nursing homes and diagnostic centres. Strange that in this age of scientific and medical wonders, the world should be sicker than ever.

Diabetes, impotency, heart disease, cancer and various viral infections ensure that our medical services are overstretched. Gone are the days when a worried parent would say 'Send for the doctor'. Now it's 'Go to the doctor' or 'Send for an ambulance'. No one is likely to come and sit by your bedside.

So I miss those doctors, now retired or long gone, who would do just that. There was Dr Jwala Prasad, for instance, a dear man who smoked quite heavily, and who owned one of the three or four cars that plied on the Mussoorie roads back in the 1960s and '70s. He was famous for his phrase 'Nothing to worry about.' No matter how ill you were, in pain or racked with a fever, he'd pat you on the shoulder and say, 'Nothing to worry about. You're going to be fine!'

And it actually helped! Such is the psychology of illness or wellness.

Another friendly neighbourhood doctor who I miss is Dr Bisht. I had only to ring him up, to tell him I was in dire straits, and ten minutes later I would hear the splutter of his old scooter as it drew up below my steps. 'Pulse is a bit fast today,' he'd say, after a brief examination. 'It's the blood pressure again. Don't tell me you have fallen in love again?'

"What's that got to do with it, doctor?'

"Falling in love always raises the blood pressure.'

In his infinite wisdom he'd hit the nail on the head — or the lover on his aching heart. The remedy? A long walk in the woods. 'Keep walking. That will do the trick.' His theory was that a little exercise was the best remedy for most ailments.

Well, the good doctor has long since retired, but the other day I met him when he was enjoying an outing with his grandchildren, and I could see that he was most anxious to do something for my well-being. At eighty, I do still occasionally fall in love, but on this occasion I had nothing to complain of—no dizziness, no irregular heartbeat, no melancholia or other symptoms of the love-sick—just a seasonal cold. So I told him I had a cold.'

"Take plenty of vitamin C,' he advised. 'And drink lots of water.' Well, I have been taking Vitamin C for a week, and I am looking like a lemon, and passed a lot of water, but a cold is a cold and it will go in its own good time.

I haven't been so lucky with dentists. As a small boy I had protruding teeth, so my mother took me to Dr Kapadia in Dehradun, a famous dentist in his time. But a painful prod from one of his instruments resulted in my screaming and kicking him on the shin. 'Take this boy away,' he told my mother. 'Don't bring him here again.' With the result that I still have protruding front teeth.

But it's better than having dentures. I have an elderly actor friend who was given the role of Count Dracula in one of those vampire films which are all the fashion these days. The trouble is, he wears dentures, false teeth, and when he grins or grimaces he doesn't look at all like a vampire.

"You'll never get those teeth into a beautiful neck,' I told him. 'We'll have to do something about them.'

So I took him to one of those street dentists who ply their trade on the outskirts of our pilgrim towns. He took out his file and sharpened my friend's false incisors until they glittered. Our hero looked like a real vampire with the sharpened incisors. But he didn't get the part. On taking the heroine into his arms and attempting to plunge his teeth into her beautiful neck, his dentures shot out and he was left toothless.

As Donald Trump would say: Sad.

Why I Miss My Less-Cash Days

In these days of cash rationing, I miss the days when I used to subsist largely on postal money orders. That was back in the days of my youth, when I freelanced from Dehradun, bombarding the country's newspapers and magazines with my articles and short stories. Magazine payments seldom exceeded ₹25 for a short story, and the publishers often found it more convenient to send these amounts by money order rather than by cheque.

I preferred it too. Better than hanging around in a bank all morning. The postman became a welcome visitor, sometimes a friend. I would sign on a printed receipt, and become the recipient of several crisp new notes, all real money, waiting to be spent. No doubt my friends would be waiting around the corner, eager to celebrate at the nearest chaat shop; but there is nothing like a little money in the pocket to boost the self-confidence of a fledgling writer.

The magazines that sent me this largesse included Sainik Samachar, the Armed Forces Weekly; Chandamama; Shankar's Weekly; The Tribune of Ambala; The Leader of Allahabad; and Baburao Patel's Mother India. Only one or two of these survive.

The Times of India and *The Statesman* were in a slightly

higher bracket as far as payments went. These amounts might seem insignificant today, but in 1956, ₹25 could buy lunches and dinners for a week.

◆

Prem, who runs a little ration shop down the road, still uses postal money order to send remittances to his aged and ailing mother in their village in a remote area of the Garhwal hills. There is no bank in the area, but the village postman makes his way to her door with a few hundred rupee notes. Let's hope he will still be able to do so.

I have always been loyal to the post office, and still use Speed Post for all my correspondence. Stamps have to be paid for in cash, so I must cut down a little on my letters. If the cash problems go on forever, I suppose postage stamps will vanish too, much to the dismay of philatelists in India and the world over, who eagerly look out for the new issues and first-day covers.

I gave up collecting long ago, but the postage stamp is part of our heritage, portraying the country's past and present.

◆

In my effort to keep up with the times I travel occasionally by plane, and the other day I thought I'd do some shopping at one of our major airports. To my dismay, the proffered credit card could not be used, as the systems 'connectivity' was down. I'm not sure what 'connectivity' means (except in the human sense) but apparently it implies some sort of electronic failure. And I hope it isn't a foretaste of things to come. If there is neither cash nor 'connectivity', what do we do for a bar of chocolate or just a magazine with which to pass the time? You just sit patiently in the airport twiddling your thumbs and gazing at your fellow travellers.

Or being gazed at.

I was sitting there meditating, or rather contemplating, when an attractive young woman came up to me and said, 'Excuse me, but are you Bejan Daruwala?'

Now I've been mistaken for various people in my life, but Bejan Daruwala was a new one.

Naturally I was flattered.

"Regretfully, no,' I answered. 'But I can tell your fortune if you like. Just show me your hand and I'll trace your life line, your head line, and your heart line.'

"No, no,' she said hastily. 'It's all right. I just thought you looked like him.'

"I won't charge anything,' I added, as an afterthought; she was probably short of cash. But she had hurried away. I don't think she trusted palmists.

An hour passed, and someone else approached me. A large lady with a small boy.

"It's so nice to see you here,' she says. 'My little boy studies one of your books in class. Will you give him your autograph?'

'Certainly ma'am.' I beam at the bright little boy. 'And what's the name of the book you are studying?'

'Tom Sawyer,' he says.

Dutifully, I sign Mark Twain on a slip of paper. Mother and son go away quite happy.

One of these days someone is going to mistake me for Ruskin Bond.

On Losing Solitude, and Discovering the Joy of Selfies

A little solitude now and then is good for the soul and good for the pen. And it is not only writers who need it. We could all do with a few hours of solitary confinement — not in a jail cell but in a room or quiet corner of our own choice. How else can we get to know ourselves?

Not everyone is in a position to renounce the material world and live in a humble dwelling on the banks of the Ganga above Rishikesh to meditate and ponder upon the meaning or absence of meaning in our transitory existence in a world that has been mismanaged by its human tenants.

Children have to be fed, marriages brokered, and cars topped up with petrol. The great saints and sages looked to the mountains for solitude. The great poets and prose-writers—Tagore, Wordsworth, Stevenson, Melville, Conrad—turned to the rivers, lakes, seas and oceans. The mountains are static, but water is always on the move, there is no stopping it.

Probably the best work in solitude was Defoe's Robinson Crusoe. Here was an intelligent man who, shipwrecked upon an uninhabited island, had solitude forced upon him. Most men would have gone mad after a year or two of complete isolation.

But Crusoe learnt to adapt to the conditions and even appreciate his enforced solitude. The arrival of Man Friday proved at first to be unsettling, but their chemistry proved to be just right, and loneliness became companionship.

Solitude is a condition appreciated only by a small minority. It seems to me that most people are scared of being left on their own, for almost every human activity is carried out on a crowded scale.

As a boy, inspired by Thoreau's Walden, I sought out a Walden pond for myself, and discovered a wilderness outside Dehradun where a hot spring emerged from a dry river-bed. I would go there often on my bicycle. There were no other visitors, just occasionally a village boy grazing his cows.

Last year I visited the same spot, although no longer on a bicycle. Hotels, restaurants, a veritable bazaar had come up on the banks of a tiny stream, but of the original hot spring there was no sign. In shock, it had probably gone underground.

In order to protect yourself from solitude or finding yourself on your own you can now equip yourself with a 'selfie' and take pictures of yourself with waterfalls and cheering crowds in the background; but take care you don't step backwards into the waterfall.

Strangely along the road below my mountain home I encountered a smart young person who wanted to take a picture of both of us with her 'selfie'. I could hardly object. So we sat on the parapet, cheek to cheek, while she attempted to get us both in the frame of her camera. All she got was her pretty left ear and my red nose, but I didn't mind, it was a long time since I'd sat cheek to cheek with a pretty young thing on a parapet wall. There's something to be said for 'selfies'.

And so I take issue with a gentleman on a TV programme

who maintained that 'selfies' were a form of narcissism, denoting some form of psychological deficiency in the owner's make-up. To me, they appear to be quite harmless fun things, provided you don't fall off a cliff or a high-rise building.

The mirror—especially that dressing-table mirror—is probably the most addictive form of narcissism, and it has been around for centuries. 'Get away from that mirror!' my aunt would scream at me whenever I lingered in front of it for several minutes, trying my best to train my hair into a puff similar to the one sported by Dev Anand or Alan Ladd or whoever was the big male star that year. Nowadays you don't see stars with puffs, possibly because they go bald rather early. Must be all this pollution.

But to return to solitude, the only place where I can find it is in my own small room looking out over the mountains. But even here I must keep my windows closed if I am not to be joined by the monkeys.

There's one particular monkey that has been looking at me speculatively through the window glass all morning. Being short-sighted I can't tell if it's a male or a female, but it makes no difference, they all have a strange desire to make off with my pyjamas. Is it because I like brightly coloured pyjamas? Or is it some sort of Freudian simian obsession which can only be explained by that psychologist on the TV channel?

Anyway, my pyjamas disappear at the rate of one a month. I have only to leave the window open for half a minute, and away goes my pyjama, over the trees and far away.

There must be a part of the forest where a whole tribe of rhesus monkeys is prancing around in my many-coloured pyjamas. They are probably having their own fashion show.

Belting around Mumbai

I have lived to see Bombay become Mumbai, Calcutta become Kolkata, and Madras become Chennai. Times change, names change, and if Bond becomes Bonda I won't object. Place-names may alter but people don't, and in Mumbai I found that people were as friendly and good-natured as ever; perhaps even more than when I was last there twenty-five years ago.

On that occasion I had travelled the Doon Express, a slow passenger train that stopped at every small station in at least five states, taking two days and two nights from Dehradun to Bombay. It had been a fairly uneventful journey, except for an incident in the small hours when we stopped at Baroda and a hand slipped through my open window, crept under my pillow, found nothing of value except my spectacles, and decided to take them anyway, leaving me to grope half-blind around Bombay until another pair could be made.

Now I curry three pairs of spectacles: one for reading, one for looking at people, and one for looking far out to sea.

On the Kingfisher flight to Mumbai, I used the second pair, as I like looking at people, especially attractive air hostesses. I found they were looking at me too, but that was because I'd caught my belt (my trouser belt, not my seat-belt) in a fellow-passenger's luggage strap and was proceeding to drag both him and his travel-bag down the aisle. We were diplomatically separated by the aforesaid air hostesses who then guided me to my seat without further mishap.

This reminded me of the occasion many years ago when I auditioned for a role in a Tarzan film.

'Who do you wish to play?' asked the casting director. 'Tarzan, of course,' I said

He gave me a long hard look. Can you swing from one tree to another?' he asked.

'Easily,' I said. 'I can even swing from a chandelier.' And I proceeded to do so, wrecking the hall they sat in, in the process. They begged me to stop.

'Thank you, Mr Bond, you have made your point. But we don't think you have the figure for the part of Tarzan. Would you like to take the part of the missionary who is being cooked to a crisp by a bunch of cannibals? Tarzan will come to your rescue.'

I declined the role with dignity.

And now I was in Mumbai, not to audition for a film, but to inaugurate the Rupa Book Festival. For old time's sake, I arrived at the venue in a horse-drawn carriage. Alighting, my recalcitrant belt-buckle got entangled with the horse's harness and I almost dragged the entire contraption into the Bajaj exhibition hall.

However, the evening's entertainment went off without a hitch. Gulzar read from Ghalib, Tom Alter read from Gulzar, Mandira Bedi read from Nandita Puri, and everyone read madly from each other, and I sat quietly in a corner to keep my belt out of further entanglements.

The next day I was taken on a tour of the city by a *Hindustan Times* journalist and a photographer. They asked me to pose on the steps of the Asiatic Society's Library, an imposing colonial edifice. While I stood there being photographed, a group of teenagers walked past and I overheard one of them remark: 'Yeh naya model hain.'

I took it as a compliment. At least they didn't call me a purana model. Perhaps there's still a chance to get that Tarzan role. If not Tarzan, then his grandfather.

The same journalist and photographer took me to a market where you could buy anything from books to bras. They thrust a thousand-rupee note into my willing hands and told me I could buy anything I liked, while they took pictures.

'Can I keep the money?' I asked. 'No, you have to spend it.'

So I bought two ladies handbags and two pairs of ladies slippers.

'For your girlfriends?' asked the journalist.

No,' I said, 'for their mothers.'

Back at the festival hall, I was presented with a beautiful sky-blue T-shirt by a charming lady who wishes to remain anonymous. I wore it the next morning when I was leaving Mumbai.

At the airport, one of the Kingfisher staff complimented on my dress sense; the first time anyone has alone so.

'Your blue shirt matches your eyes,' she said.

After that, I shall definitely fly Kingfisher again.

Monkey on the Roof

Quite often, I'm up with the lark—more often, with the sound of monkeys jumping on my tin roof. I've often wondered why hill-station houses must have these rusty red tin roofs, apart from an understandable human desire to make them look like battered old biscuit tins. Well, now I know. They are there for the benefit of monkeys, langurs, field-rats, cats, crows, mynas, spiders and scorpions.

I don't mind the spiders—they seem harmless enough. The scorpions are evil-looking but sluggish—unlike the dashing red scorpions of the Rajasthan desert. The other day I found a scorpion enjoying a nap on my pillow. I like to have my pillow to myself, so I tipped the slumbering creature out of the window and returned to my afternoon siesta. I do not take the lives of fellow creatures if I can help it. Cats are not so squeamish. At night they get between the tin roof and the wooden ceiling and create havoc among the rats and mice who dwell there. And early morning, if I leave a window open, the monkeys will finish anything they find on the breakfast table.

In spite of occasional rude awakenings, I enjoy sleeping late, especially on winter mornings when the sun struggles to penetrate banks of cloud or mist or drizzle. The bed is one of my favourite places. And even if I am wide awake, I can lie there under the blanket and razai and enjoy the view without rising. The window in front of me looks out on the clouds or the clear sky; the window beside it gives me a view of upper Landour and the houses on the slopes; and the far window looks out on a thicket of oak trees. And if I sit up in bed, I can see the road and some of the people on it.

But to start with my bed, for that's where the day begins and ends. There's something to be said for beds. After all, we spend roughly half our lives stretched out upon them. The amount of time spent in sleep varies from one individual to another.

Five hours sleepeth a traveller, seven a scholar, eight a merchant, and eleven every knave.

So goes an old proverb, and there is much truth in proverbs. I must fall somewhere between merchant and knave. There are times when I like to rise early and times when I enjoy sleeping late. If I fall asleep before midnight, I will rise early. One hour's sleep before midnight is worth two after. When the moon is up, the night has its magic; but at two or three in the morning there is very little to offer, because by ten even cats, bats and field-rats are asleep. In summer, bird-song starts at dawn, somewhere between four and five o'clock and that's a good time to be up and about, exercising mind or body.

The other morning I was up at five; wrote a couple of pages, opened my window and swallowed a portion of cloud; closed it, conscience clear, and returned to bed where presently a cup of tea materialised, prepared by Beena or Dolly or some other member of the family. But for that morning cup of tea, would I have survived all these years? Without it, the mornings would be one long, endless wasteland. Without it, I would not get up. I would refuse breakfast, lunch and dinner, and waste away. Looking back upon my life from the vantage point of seventy years, I cannot remember a time when I was deprived of that morning cup of tea. Except for when I was in boarding school. Now you know why I ran away.

Getting up and making my own tea is no fun either. It has to be brought to me by some gentle soul-man, woman or child—who has got up before everyone else in order to ensure that I get up too.

The best tea I've ever drunk was made by an ex-convict who worked for my landlady in Dehradun, many years ago. He told me that while he was in jail he was assigned to the task of making the warden's tea. It was appreciated so much that they wouldn't let him go even after he'd served his sentence. How, then, did he gain his freedom? Well, my landlady was the wife of the jail superintendent. So you see how well the system worked!

For a while in London, I had a Jewish landlady who brought me my breakfast on a tray. I don't know if such civilised courtesies still exist. Back in the 1950s, English food was not very exciting; it had yet to be enriched by Indian curries and Chinese noodles. But breakfasts were always good—far superior to the skimpy fare served out by the French. Bacon and eggs, marmalade on toast, occasionally a kipper, a sausage, a slice of ham, grapefruit... what more could anyone ask for at the start of a busy day? And even now, when the days aren't quite so busy, I might skip lunch or dinner but I'll breakfast well.

So finally I'm out of bed and enjoying my breakfast. The children have gone to school and silence has descended on the house. A day in the life of Ruskin Bond is about to commence. I am at liberty to write a poem or a story or fill these pages with inconsequential thoughts. But first I must get dressed.

I am not fond of clothes, but I wouldn't care to start the day's work without at least wearing a clean shirt. When I was a struggling young writer, I did not possess more than two shirts at one time, but I would wash one every night in the hope that it would be dry by morning. Even today, I don't have a large wardrobe. It isn't possible, not with all these monkeys around. If you see a large red monkey wearing a blue and yellow check bush-shirt, please try and retrieve it for me; it's my favourite shirt. Putting clothes out on the roof to dry is fairly common practice in hill-stations, but not to be recommended. Only the other day, when a strong wind came up from the east, I saw my pyjamas floating away downhill to end up entangled in the branches of an oak tree. Fortunately the milkman's son, who is good at climbing oak trees, rescued them for me. The milkman's son does not pass his exams, but as long as he can climb trees, he'll be a success in life. All of us need just one good accomplishment in order to get by. Obviously he can't spend the rest of his life climbing trees, but it's the agility and enterprise involved in the act that will make him a survivor.

Enough of bed and breakfast and getting ready for the long morning's journey into day. When does this ageing writer sit down to write? Or does he simply dictate to a secretary or into a machine of some kind? Well, I wish that was the case, because I'm a lazy sort of writer, better in bed than out of it. Unfortunately, I get tongue-tied when I try to tell a story, make a speech, or conduct something as simple as a telephone or cell phone conversation.

Recently Dolly made me buy a mobile phone; it would make me more efficient and up-to-date, she said. I tried making a call, and when nothing happened, she said, 'Dada, you're holding it upside down!' I got it the right way up and tried again, and when nothing happened, she said, 'Not here. You have to go to the window.'

I dutifully walked over and tried again. No luck. 'Open the window,' ordered Dolly. I opened the window. Just a crackle on the cell phone. 'Now look out of the window!' I looked out, and there were all these schoolgirls gazing up at me, wondering why I was staring down at them. 'Good morning girls,' I called out, and gave them a friendly wave. 'No girls here,' said a gruff voice on the cell phone. 'This is your local thana.'

I gave the mobile to Dolly. She has no difficulty in getting through to her friends, or hearing from them. I'm no good at these things, except to pay the bill.

I'm strictly a man of the written word. Give me pen and paper and I manage to get something down, even if it's only for my own amusement. An elderly reader once remarked, 'How do you manage to write so much about nothing?' to which I could only reply: 'Well, it's better than writing nothing about everything!'

That small red ant walking across my desk may mean nothing to the world at large, but to me it represents the world at large. It represents industry, single-mindedness, intricacy of design, the perfection of nature, the miracle of creation. So much so, that it inspires me to poetic composition:

> You stride through the wasteland of my desk,
> Pressing on over books and papers,
> Down the wall and across the floor
> Small red ant, now crossing a sea of raindrops
> At my open door.
> Your destiny, your task
> To carry home

That heavy sunflower seed,
   Waving it like a banner
   Of victory!

Nothing is insignificant; nothing is without consequence in the intricate web of life.

And in the Loo

I am fairly tolerant about these monkeys doing the bhangra on my roof, but I do resent it when they start invading my rooms. Not so long ago, I opened the bathroom door to find a very large Rhesus monkey sitting on the potty. He wasn't actually using the potty—monkeys prefer parapet walls—but he had obviously found it a comfortable place to sit, and he showed no signs of vacating the throne when politely requested to do so. Bullies seldom do. So I had to give him a fright by slamming the door as loudly as I could, and he took off through the open window and found his cousins on the hillside.

On another occasion, a female of the species sat on my desk, lifted the telephone receiver and appeared to be making an STD call to some distant relative. Some ladies are apt to linger long over their calls, and I hated to interrupt, but I was anxious to get in touch with my publisher, who took priority; so I pushed her off my desk with a feather-duster. She was so resentful of this intrusion that she made off with my telephone directory and tore it to shreds, scattering pages along the road. As this was something that I had wanted to do for a long time, I could not help admiring her audacity.

The kitchen area of our flat is closely guarded, as I resent sharing my breakfast with creatures great and small. But the other day a wily crow flew in and made off with my boiled egg. I know crows are fond of eggs—other birds' eggs that is—but I did not know that they like them boiled. Anyway, this egg was still piping hot, and the crow had to drop it on the road, where it was seized upon by one of the stray dogs who police this end of the road.

Barking furiously, the dogs run after the monkeys, who simply leap onto the nearest tree or rooftop and proceed to throw insults at the frustrated pack. The dogs never succeed in catching anything except their own kind. Canine intruders from another area are readily attacked and driven away.

♦

Having dressed, breakfasted and written the morning's two or three pages (early morning is the best time to do this), I am free to walk up the road to the bank or post office or tea shop at the top of the hill. If it's springtime, I shall look out for wildflowers. If it's monsoon time; I shall look out for leeches.

Well, it's monsoon time, and we haven't seen the sun for a couple of weeks Clouds envelop the hills, and a light shower is falling. I have unfurled my bright yellow umbrella, as a gesture of defiance. At least it provides some contrast to the grey sky and the dark green of the hillside. You cannot see the snows or even the next mountain.

There's no one else on the road today, only a few intrepid tourists from Amritsar I overhead one robust Punjabi complain to his guide: You've brought us all the way to the top of this forsaken mountain, and what have you shown us? The kabristan!

True, the old British graves are all that one can see through the fog. Some of the tombstones have been standing there for close on two centuries. The old abandoned parsonage next door to the cemetery is now the home of Victor Banerjee the celebrated actor. He enjoys living next door to the graveyard, and one night he defied me to walk home alone past the graves. I am not a supersticious person but I did feel rather uneasy as those old graves loomed up through the mist. I was startled by the cry of a night-bird emanating from behind one of the tombstones. Then a weird, blood-chilling cry rose from a clump of bushes. It was Victor, trying to frighten me—or possibly practicing for his next role as Dracula. I was about to break into a run when a large dog—one of our strays—appeared beside me and accompanied me home. On a dark and scary night, even a half-starved mongrel is welcome company.

By day, the road holds no terrors. But there are other hazards. On the road near Char Duskan, several small boys are kicking a football around. The ball rolls temptingly towards me. Remembering my football skills of fifty or more years ago, I cannot resist the temptation to put boot to ball. I give it a mighty kick. The ball sails away, the children applaud, I am left hopping about on the road in agony, I had quite forgotten my gout!

I'm glad I stuck to writing instead of taking up professional football. At seventy I can still write without inflicting damage on myself.

◆

When I am feeling good, and have the road to myself, I do occasionally break into song. This is the only opportunity I have to sing. Otherwise my musical abilities turn friends into foes.

I am not permitted to sing in the homes of my friends. If I am being driven about in their cars, I am told to remain silent unless we veer off the road or hit an oncoming vehicle. Even at home, the sound of my music causes the girls to drop dishes and the children to find an excuse to stop doing their homework.

'Dada is ill again,' says Gautam, when all I am trying to do is emulate Caruso singing 'Che Gelida Manina' (Your Tiny Hand is Frozen) from *La Bohéme*. Our tiny hands do freeze up here in the winter, and there's nothing like an operatic aria to get the blood circulating freely. Of course Caruso was a tenor, but I can also sing baritone like Domingo or Nelson Eddy and bass like Chaliapin the great Russian singer. Sometimes I combine all three voices-tenor, baritone, bass and that's when the window glass shatters and cars come to a screeching halt.

It was a boyhood ambition to be an opera star, but I'm afraid I never made it beyond the school choir. Our music teacher did not appreciate the wide range of my voice.

'Too loud!' she would screech. 'Too flat!'

'Caruso sings in A-flat,' I replied.

'You sound like a warbling frog,' she snapped.

'And you look like one,' I responded.

And that was the end of my brief appearance in cassock and surplice.

But when I'm on the open road—especially when it's raining and I have the road to myself—I am free to sing as loud and as flat as I like, and if flat tyres on passing cars are the result, it's the fault of the tyres and not my singing.

So here we go:

When you are down and out,
Lift up your head and shout
'It's going to be a great day!'

There's nothing like a spirited song to raise the flagging spirit. Whenever I feel down and out—and that's often enough—I recall some old favourite and share it with the trees, the birds, and even those pesky monkeys.

> 'Just like a sunflower
> After a summer shower
> My inspiration is you!'

Sloppy, sentimental stuff, but it works.

And there's always the likelihood of a little romance arou the corner.

> 'Some enchanted evening
> You will see a stranger
> Across a crowded room...'

Actually, I prefer the winding road to a crowded road Romantic encounters are more likely when there are not many people around. Such as the other day, when I unfurled my new umbrella and was sauntering up the road singing my favourite rain song, 'Singing in the Rain'.

I had gone some distance when I noticed a young lady struggling up the road a little way ahead of me. My glasses were wet and misty, but I was determined to share my umbrella with any damsel in distress. So, huffing and puffing, I caught up with her.

'Do share my umbrella,' I offered.

No, she wasn't sweet twenty-one, as I'd hoped. She nearer eighty. But she was munching on a bhutta, so her teeth were in good order. She took the umbrella from me a munched on ahead, leaving me to get drenched. A retired headmistress, as I discovered later!

She returned the umbrella when we got to Char Dukan, in future I shall make a frontal approach before making gallant overtures on the road. Those crowded rooms are safer.

Monsoon time, and umbrellas are taken out and frequently lost. I lost three last year. One was borrowed, and as you know, borrowed books and umbrellas are seldom returned. By some mysterious process they become the permanent property of the borrower. Another disappeared while I was cashing a cheque in the bank. And the third was wrecked in the following fashion.

Coming down from Char Dukan, I found two hefty boys engaged in furious combat in the middle of the road. One was a kick-boxer, the other a kung-fu exponent. Afraid that one of them would be badly hurt, I decided to intervene, and called out, 'Come on boys, break it up! I thrust my umbrella between them in a bid to end the fracas. My umbrella received a mighty kick, and went sailing across the road and over the parapet. The boys stopped fighting in order to laugh at my discomfiture. One of them retrieved my umbrella, minus its handle.

In a way, I'd been successful as a peacemaker-certainly more successful than the United Nations—although at some cost to my personal property. Well, we peacemakers must be prepared to put up with a little inconvenience.

I'm a great believer in the Law of Compensation (as propounded by Emerson in his famous essay)—that what we do, good or bad, is returned in full measure in this life rather than in the hereafter.

Not long after the incident just described, there was my old friend Vipin Buckshey standing on the threshold with a seasonal gift—a beautiful blue umbrella!

He did not know about the street-fighter, but had read my story *The Blue Umbrella*—a simple tale about greed being overcome by generosity—and had bought me a blue umbrella in appreciation. I shall be careful not to lose it.

And at the Bank

Yes, those monkeys are at the bank too. They are there before it opens, doing their best to damage the roof; and they are there when it closes, tearing up the geraniums so lovingly planted by the manager.

I am also there when it opens, having, as usual, run over the weekend, with the result that all I have in my pocket is a damaged fifty rupee note which I have attempted to with Sellotape.

The bank opens promptly at ten a.m. Unfortunate doesn't have any money. No, it has not collapsed like the Mansaram Bank, for which Ganesh Saili still has his fa chequebook showing a balance of three hundred rupe 1957; the taxi with the cash (which comes from the branch) has been caught in a traffic jam duet unprecedented influx of tourists. This happens occasionally, as there are only two ways in and out of Mussoorie and only one way to Char Dukan.

Anyway, I pass the time by having a cup of tea with the manager and discussing the latest cricket test match with the cashier.

He is of the opinion that the result of a match depends on who wins the toss, while I maintain that the game is won by the team that has slept better the night before.

The cash arrives safely and I emerge into the sunshine to be met by several small boys who demand money for a cricket ball. I part with a new fifty rupee note (the old one having been obligingly changed by the cashier) and then run into several members of Tom Alter's cricket team, who insist that I join their Invitation XI in a game against the Dhobi Ghat Team, about to be played up at Chey-Tanki flat. (This was before the area got fenced off by the Defence establishment as cricket balls kept sailing into their offices and smashing their computers.) :

Forgetting my age, but remembering my great days as a twelfth man for the Doon Heroes, I consented on condition that a substitute would field in my place. (No longer would I be a twelfth man.)

Well, the Dhobi Ghat Team put up a good score, and Tom's Invitation XI was trailing by some sixty or seventy runs, when I came in to bat at number seven. Tom was at the other end, holding the innings together.

The bowler (who ran a dry-cleaner's in town) was a real speedster, and his first ball caught me in the midriff. I am well padded there (by nature) but I resolved not to use that dry cleaner's shop again. The second ball took the edge of my bat and sped away for four.

Well played, Ruskin! called Tom encouragingly, and I resolved to write a part for him in my next story

I tapped the third ball into the covers and set off for a run, completely forgetting that I hadn't taken a run in fifty years. Still, I got to the other end, gasping for breath and trembling in the legs. Next, Tom tapped the ball away and called me for a run! There was no way I was going to join the brave souls sleeping in Jogger's Park (the name for the Landour cemetery), so I held up my hand and remained rooted to the crease. Tom was half-way down the pitch when the ball hit his stumps and he was run out. The look he gave me as he marched back to the pavilion was as effective as any that he had essayed in his more villainous roles.

I managed another streaky four before being bowled, and when I returned to the 'pavilion' (the gardener's shed), Tom sportingly said, You should stick to writing, Ruskin'—quite forgetting that I had out-scored him!

After that, I had to pay for the refreshments and contribute towards the prize money (won by the Dhobi Ghat Team), and all this necessitated another trip to the bank before closing time.

◆

I was home well in time for lunch. My favourite rajma-bean curry, with hot chapattis and mango pickle. As it was a Saturday, the kids were home from school, and we all tucked in—except for Gautam who was on a hunger-strike because his promised Saturday ice cream was missing. Then his father arrived and took us for a drive to Dhanaulti, where there was ice cream aplenty.

Gone are the days when a picnic involved preparing and packing a lunch basket, and then trudging off into the wilderness on a hot and dusty road. People don't walk anymore. They get into their cars and drive out to a crowded 'picnic spot' where dhabas will provide you with national dishes such as chowmein or pizzas. While Indian cuisine has taken over Britain, Chinese and Italian dishes have conquered Indian palates. There's globalisation for you.

But I miss those picnics of old. They were leisurely, strung-out affairs. We seemed to have more time on our hands and a picnic meant an entire day's outing.

In Simla we picnicked at the Brockhurst tennis courts (now apartment buildings), or out at Jutogh or Summer Hill, or beyond Chota Simla; but not at Jakko, where the monkeys hundreds of them—were inclined to join in.

In Dehradun we picnicked at Sulphur Springs, or in the hills near Rajpura, or on the banks of the Tons or Suswa rivers. You could also go fishing at Raiwala, just before the Song joins the Ganga. Equipped with rod and line, some friends and I went fishing there, but being inexpert, caught nothing. Some soldiers who were camping there had caught dozens of fish (by stunning them with explosives, I'm afraid and were generous enough to give us a couple of large singharas. We returned to Dehra with our 'catch', and impressed friends and neighbours with our prowess as anglers.

Here in Mussoorie there was Mossy Falls, and other more distant falls: the Company Bagh, Clouds End, Haunted House: and the banks of the little Aglar river.

I won't go down to the Aglar again, at least not on foot Climbing up, ascending from 2,000 to 7,000 feet within a distance of three or four miles takes it out of you. On my first visit, some thirty years ago, I was accompanied by severa school children. On our way back, we took the wrong path and lost our way (a frequent occurrence when I'm put in charge), and it was past ten o'clock when we were located by a bunch of anxious and angry parents accompanied by villager who'd seen me going down. Fortunately, there was a full moon and there were no mishaps on the steep and stony path.

We went to bed hungry that night.

On another occasion, well provisioned with parathas various sabzi, pickles, boiled eggs and bananas, two young friends— Kuku and Deepak—and I, tramped down to the Aglar and spread ourselves out on a grassy knoll. A pool of limpid water looked cool and inviting. We removed our clothes and plunged into the water. Great fun! We romped about quite oblivious to what might be happening to our provisions Then one of us looked up and yelled, 'Monkeys!' At least six of them were tucking into our lunch. We scrambled up the bank, and the monkeys fled, taking with them the remains of the parathas, the last bananas, and most of our underwear. They had left the pickle for us.

We were a sorry-looking threesome by the time we returned to the town. But we did not go to bed hungry. We had enough money between us for a meal at Neelam's—then the most popular restaurant on the Mall—and we did full justice to various kababs, koftas, tikkas and tandoori rotis.

◆

By now my readers will have come to the conclusion that I am perpetually persecuted by monkeys. And you would not be far wrong, gentle reader. Even as I write, I see one grinning at me from my window. Fortunately the window is closed and he cannot get in. I stick my tongue out at him, and he takes off, finding me far more hideous than his friends and relations

But it wasn't always like that. Some years ago, when I lived in Maplewood, on the edge of the forest, a little girl monkey would sometimes perch shyly on the windowsill and study me with friendly curiosity. The rest of her tribe showed no interest in me as a person, but this little girl-and I think of her as a human rather than as a monkey-would turn up every morning while I was at my typewriter, and sit there quietly, her eyes intent on me as I tapped out a story or article. Perhaps it was the typewriter that fascinated her. I like to think it was my blue eyes. She had blue eyes too!

Now it isn't often that girls take a fancy to me, but I like to think that the little monkey had a crush on me. Her eyes had a gentle, appealing look, and she would make little chuckling sounds that I took for intimate conversation. If I approached, she would leap onto the walnut tree just outside the window and gesture to me to join her there. But my tree-climbing days were already over; and besides, I was afraid of her peers and parents.

One day I came into the room and found her at the typewriter, playing with the keys. When she saw me, she returned to the window and looked guilty. I looked down at the sheet in my machine. Had she been trying to give me a message? It read something like this—*!;!_1;:0—and there it broke off. I'm convinced she was trying to write the word 'love'.

However, I never did find out for sure, and the tribe went away, taking my girl friend with her. I never saw her again. Perhaps they married her off.

◆

Talking of marriages, I am often asked by sympathetic readers why I never married. Now that's a long, sad story which would be out of place here, but I can tell you the story of my Uncle Bertie and why he never married.

As a young man, Uncle Bertie worked at the Ishapore rifle factory, which is just outside Kolkata. In pre-Independence days, Ishapore had a large Anglo-Indian and European community, many of whom were employed in the factory. Uncle Bertie was an impetuous fellow. He had a bit of a fling with a girl who lived across the road, and after a romp in the nearest mango-grove, he asked her to marry him. She agreed with alacrity. She was older than him, much taller, and her figure—46, 46, 46—would have been the envy of Marlene Dietrich or Marilyn Monroe. The girl's parents were agreeable, and everything had been arranged when Bertie Bond began to have second thoughts. He was always one for second thoughts. His brief infatuation over, he began to wonder what he had seen in the girl in the first place. She liked going to dances and Bertie couldn't dance. Her reading was limited to film magazines such as *Hollywood Romance,* while Bertie read Maxim Gorky and Emile Zola. She could not cook. Nor could Bertie. And khansamas were expensive. She liked to go shopping and Bertie's salary was three hundred rupees per month.

The banns were announced, the great day came around, and the church filled up with friends, relatives and well wishers. The padre put on his gown and prepared to take the wedding service. The bride was present, arrayed in the white wedding dress in which her mother had been married. But there was no sign of Bertie. Half an hour, an hour, two hours passed. The bridegroom could not be found.

He had, in fact, fled to Calcutta, and had gone underground. He remained underground for sometime, emerging from hiding only in order to take a job at the docks in Ishapore. Everyone was waiting for him to return. They had varied and interesting ideas of what they would do to him. Some of them are still waiting

'Marriage,' said Oscar Wilde, 'is a romance in which the hero dies in the first chapter.'

Uncle Bertie made his exit in the Preface.

Granny's Tree-Climbing

Granny was a genius. You'd like to know why?
Because she could climb trees. Spreading or high,
She'd be up their branches in a trice. And mind you,
When last she climbed a tree she was sixty-two.

Ever since childhood, she'd had this gift
For being happier in a tree than in a lift;
And though, as time went by, she would be told
That climbing trees should stop when one grew old—
And that growing old should be gone about gracefully—
She'd laugh and say, 'Well, I'll grow old disgracefully!
I can do it better.' And we had to agree;
For in all the garden there wasn't a tree
She hadn't been up at one time or another—
(Having learned to climb from a loving brother
When she was six)—but it was feared by all
That one day she'd suffer a terrible fall.

The outcome was different—while we were in town
She climbed a tree and couldn't come down!
She remained on her perch until we came home,
We fetched her a ladder, and she came down alone.

As she looked a bit shaken, we sent for out doc,
Who said, 'She is fine—just a bit of a shock.'
He took Granny's temperature. 'Some fever,' he said;
'I strongly recommend a quiet week in bed.'

We sighed with relief and tucked her up well—
Poor Granny! It was just like a season in hell:
Confined to her bedroom, while every breeze
Murmured of summer and dancing leaves...
But she held her peace till she felt stronger,
Then sat up and said, 'I'll lie here no longer!'
She called for my father and told him undaunted
That a house in a tree-top was what she now wanted.
My Dad knew his duty. He said, 'That's all right—
'You'll have what you want—I shall start work tonight.'

With my expert assistance, he soon finished the chore,
Made her a tree-house with windows and a door.
So Granny moved up; and now, everyday,
I go to her room with glasses and a tray.
She sits there in state and drinks cocktails with me,
Upholding her right to reside in a tree.

[Written for Grandmothers' Rights Everywhere]